BRUTAL DAYS

A DARK HIGH SCHOOL BULLY ROMANCE

HIDDEN VALLEY ELITE
BOOK THREE

ISLA VAUGHN

ARROWSCOPE PRESS, LLC

CHAPTER ONE

SKYLAR

#Goals

"Our senior year is going to be epic." My best friend, Gia Moretti, was pumped and determined to shed her band geek, tuba-playing image.

Of the two of us, I was the rebel, with black clothes and leather, but underneath, I was a regular person who knew myself. Rebelling wasn't all Gia thought it was. We were polar opposites, but she was my ride-or-die bestie, and I would do anything for her.

I always thought her insecurity was just in her head. With her loving family and a homey and typical house, she had every-thing I wished for. *And the v-card obsession?* It wasn't that big a deal. But to Gia, it was huge. She had a list, which she would tell me in great detail, whether I agreed to hear it or not.

"Listen up, my friend," Gia gushed, "my four-point plan is fabulous and on a strict timeline. I will achieve these goals every quarter of my senior year."

"What's the plan?" I flopped onto my stomach on her lilac bedspread to see the poster she had taped inside the closet door she'd just opened. I would regret asking, but it was important to her.

"I can tell you're not taking this seriously." Gia's hands found her generous hips.

I grinned and shifted to sit cross-legged on her bed. "I am."

"As I've said before, I don't want to spend my senior year as a band geek. I've done that for three years, and I've never been on a date or had a real kiss, and I'm still a virgin."

"I'm a virgin too. It's not that big a deal."

Gia narrowed her dark eyes at me, and I laughed.

"Okay, I'm sorry. Go on."

"Here's my four-point plan. Number one"—she tapped her poster at the appropriate purple-Sharpie-written spot—"get invited to the Ring."

The Ring was the underground fight club where all the "cool kids," as Gia put it, hung out.

I'd been there before, and I hadn't been impressed. "What's the next one?"

"Number two, get a popular boyfriend."

Overrated. "Why does he have to be popular? Marty Winston has been in love with you since fifth grade."

"Please. He's four foot two."

"So what?" I'd never understood her obsession with height regardless of temperament. Marty was sweet, a characteristic at the top of my list of must-haves for a guy.

Gia glared, her disapproving mouth set in a straight line. "Because I'm five-six and fat. I want someone who makes me feel small and delicate."

"Stop saying you're fat. That's not true." I hated when she put herself down. "You're curvy in all the right places. And anyone who says otherwise is an asshole. Listen to me, not jerk-offs."

She ignored me. "Number three, lose my v-card."

"Oh my God, Gia. It's not like it's a disease."

"And finally, become prom queen." She grinned, her excitement almost contagious.

"Why?" I was truly horrified by that last one.

I never could understand her fixation on being popular. My mom had been, and it had gotten her literally nothing. She was a single parent who struggled to make ends meet. I had to breathe through my frustration because the truth was that Gia had been my friend since third grade, when my dad punched me in the face. Gia had found me hiding in her backyard, bruised and crying. Because of that, I would support her, starting with the pre-first-day-of-school barbecue at Phoenix and Shane Bennett's house. It was after the football team's afternoon practice, and Gia really wanted to go.

"How did you get invited to the barbecue?" Those guys didn't hang out with band kids.

Gia laughed and flicked her long, curly hair over her shoulder. "We're crashing it." Her eyes sparkled with excitement. "The secret to a party like that is to act like we belong. And this is their end-of-summer party. So many people will be there that no one will even notice us."

Fuck my life. The things I will do for her... "Fine." I scooted off her bed and stood. "But I have to cover the football practice for the school blog." I hated it.

Every school had one, even Hidden Valley Academy. And thanks to my creative writing teacher, who thought I should be a journalist, I'd been assigned. I hated sports with the passion of a thousand burning suns. But it wasn't like I had a choice. Besides, writing was how I had hacked my way onto the student list at the academy.

"We can meet after and get ready to go then."

I left Gia, who had turned to go through her closet to start the crazy process where she discarded clothes she deemed not good enough in heaps on her bed. If I could get through the next few hours, I could zone out in front of my TV and forget about all the drama. That day had just been a lot. I said bye to Gia's mom and headed out, resigned to what I needed to do. I would support Gia and be there for her because that was what best friends did. *But I have a really bad feeling about this.*

CHAPTER TWO

DAMON

#SeniorYearBaby

Adrenaline pumped through me, and I pounded once on Shane's helmet. "Senior year." I couldn't help grinning.

It was our last year at Hidden Valley Academy before we would move on to Thane. The college wasn't too far from where we lived in Santa Monica, California, and my brother was already there kicking ass and taking names. Goddamn, did I miss him. It wasn't the same with just the three of us here.

"Hell, yeah!" Phoenix took off his helmet and slapped me on the back, which I hardly felt under all the pads.

My cousin, Phoenix, had the coveted QB position, which was fine with me because I was an all-state running back. Shane, too, even though he volleyed between wide receiver and defense. Phoenix was a legend. Lucky for him, he had options to pass the ball to—Shane and me. I loved the thrill of the game. It made sense and fed my need to annihilate whoever was in my way on the field. And when I had the ball, which I should if it wasn't in the air, I could bust through tackles like no one else.

"Let's get moving so we can head to the barbecue at your house. Need me to pick anything up on my way there?" I asked.

Phoenix and Shane threw the party we were heading to and a Fourth of July one every year. Their mom, our aunt Cece, was cool with it. She usually crashed at our place during the day when they held one. So long as the place was cleaned up and no one got injured or died, she was cool with it—the product of being a single parent and overworked ER nurse.

"Nah, we're good. Shane managed most of the party prep. I appreciate your contribution to the cooking staff. I wasn't looking forward to grilling the mountain of meat my brother got from the store."

"No problem. I want to party with you guys, not stand by the grill just to talk to you."

We headed off the field, and my gaze inevitably went to the chick in the stands that'd been screwing with me all morning, taking pictures and notes. She was smoke-show hot, and I got the impression she didn't care about her appearance based on the overly large black glasses that matched the color of her long hair. They didn't hide her cornflower-blue eyes, high cheekbones, or perfect bee-stung mouth. She wore black leggings that left nothing to the imagination and a tight blue shirt with strategic tears to show the black cami under it.

Her entire look did things to me that no girl had managed to. Awareness crackled in the air as I closed the distance to where she stood. She would do for the night. I had energy to burn and needed sex like my next breath. It was that or fight. Darkness swirled inside me, needing an outlet all the time. Football helped take the edge off, but I'd been spiraling, my lack of control growing ever since Mom died and I'd learned what I had about my dad that day.

My brother was right. Our dad was an asshole. It wasn't just our mom at the root of all the family drama. And because of that, I had to find an outlet, or I would lash out. *The worst part?* I feared I was more like my dad than I'd ever known. No girl held my interest, and I tended to treat them terribly.

The chick stared at me as I neared, and I felt an unmistakable pull I couldn't ignore. So I didn't. I stopped in front of her, and my gaze caressed her body from head to toe and back again.

"Come to the barbecue with me." It wasn't a question. I never needed to ask. If I gave any girl attention, she fell in line like an overeager puppy.

Her mouth dropped open, and I imagined what I would like to do with those lips, then adjusted myself because, goddamn, she was gorgeous.

She laughed before wiping the amusement from her face. "I think not."

I couldn't have heard her right. I took in her notepad and camera. She better not have been taking pictures of my cousins and not me. "What are you doing here?"

"I have the unfortunate job of writing a piece for the school's blog about today's practice. I planned to go with an article dedicated to you."

I grinned, dark thoughts swirling in my mind of what I could show her—and not on the field. "I can show you a lot more."

"Yeah, I don't think so. How's it going with Cole off at Thane? I mean, you're the smaller, less talented Savage brother. Is the pressure off this year?"

Interesting. I'd never had a girl not fall in line when I snapped my fingers. I studied her more closely. She looked familiar. "You're Skylar McCormick. You were in my math class last year."

She'd said no to a date with me last year too.

"Yep."

A slow grin curved her lips, and I couldn't help but look at them again.

"And now you're remembering that you asked me out last year." She tsked. "You crashed and burned again."

"That never happens. You must either swing for the other team, or you're afraid."

"Sorry to bruise your fragile ego." She stuck out her lower lip in a pouty face. "Back to the article. This wasn't your best practice. You fumbled a ball, missing a chance for a touchdown. Do you prefer the hashtag dumb jock or butterfingers?"

What the fuck is this chick's problem? I couldn't figure her out. "If you print something that makes me look bad, I promise you'll regret it."

She made a face then stepped around me and descended the bleachers before walking off the field. I followed her progress, eyes narrowed. I would find out what her issue was. It wasn't an option. The chick intrigued me too much.

"That didn't look like it went well," Shane said, his helmet tucked under his arm.

Phoenix's dangled from his fingertips as he came to stand on the other side of me. We stood watching as Skylar walked away. I fought the urge to follow, tempted by the sway of her hips.

"Who is she?" Shane asked.

"She's nobody, and if she prints something shitty about me, I'll make sure she pays for it too."

CHAPTER THREE

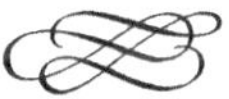

SKYLAR

#OntheProwl

Gia was on a mission, which meant I was too. We were on the prowl to catch a guy who could hit all four of her goals. That wouldn't be difficult with her outfit of a silky dusky-blue cami that I swore was a nightshirt from Victoria's Secret paired with shorts so short I could see Gia's religion when she bent down. And she wore heels. Not me. I wore my standard I-don't-give-a-fuck outfit of ripped jeans and a flannel tied over a tight white tee.

We stood by the pool in the twins' backyard, a White Claw in Gia's hand and water in mine. She hadn't been kidding about how easy it was to slip in among the crowd. And I hadn't shared the tidbit of how I'd been invited. It was her thing, her checklist, and I only came to support her and help her get it started.

The smell of hamburgers and hot dogs wafted through the air. Music and laughter escalated in waves, but I would prefer to hear the actual waves. Gia fed off the revelry, but I wanted to escape. Time to get it over with. I scanned the crowd for possibilities.

Tim Stone stood by the coolers, and I nudged Gia. "What about Tim? He's on the debate team and actually nice."

"No." She took a sip then rearranged her thick curls to fall over her shoulder.

"Jeff Anderson? He's cute and in my journalism class."

She rolled her eyes, refusing to comment.

Fine. "Sam Lewison. He's popular and involved in student council."

"Absolutely not." She grabbed my arm and looked at me with an intensity that drove home how important her plan was to her. "I need a prom king, a guy who already has the senior class in his pocket so I can slide into girlfriend space and be adored as his queen."

"That sounds like a nightmare."

She huffed. "It is to you, but to me… it's everything. I want this, Sky."

The unfamiliar ground left me desperately wanting to go home. The press of bodies made my skin itch, and way too many jocks and cheerleaders ambled about. It wasn't my scene, and I hated the people there. I had gone to the academy in the first place for its stellar writing program and because Gia was there.

I turned toward the gate, wondering if she would miss me if I bolted to the beach. "This is silly." I stepped in the direction of salvation.

"Sky, come on," Gia pleaded and latched onto my arm, holding me in place. "Please stay and help."

Everything in me stilled. I couldn't have moved if I'd wanted to. Tall, dark, and devastatingly handsome just walked into the party through the gate where I had been plotting my escape. Damon Savage. I had talked a big game with him earlier, but the truth was, he affected me too much.

For Christ's sake, he looked like he'd stepped out of a magazine.

From the corner of my eye, I noticed Gia nodding. "Oh, yeah. That's him."

Sheer panic raced through my blood, and I whirled to face her. "No. You can't be serious."

"The name Savage is apt for those boys." Gia licked her lips.

My mouth fell open. She looked like she planned to eat him up. I couldn't let her do it. "Gia, he's an asshole of the worst kind. You *need* to find someone else. You won't get him to do anything you want. Trust me."

She turned heavy-lidded eyes that swirled deviously with whatever plot she had concocted. "You agreed to help, and that's the guy. And"—she glanced to where Damon had stopped—"you need to help me separate him from the herd."

Her bad idea had disaster written all over it. With no choice, I approached Damon with her. Dark-blue eyes swung our way and locked on me. I felt trapped and panicky, especially because I hadn't told Gia about what had happened earlier in the day. She would be devastated if she found out Damon hit on me. Not that I would act on anything from a dumb jock.

A slow, dangerous smile settled on his chiseled face.

She can't be serious. Damon is a predator.

The closer we got, the more my stomach churned. *Will he say something about earlier?* I should have told her, but it had been such a no-go in my book that I hadn't thought it mattered. Yet, suddenly it did. With Gia's sights set on one of the fucking Elite —the top guys at our school, football stars that our peers treated like gods—there would be no convincing her otherwise.

What happened next was the stuff of nightmares. Gia's heel caught on the edge of the travertine tile. I saw from the corner of my eye and turned to grab her, but it was too late. Or too late for Damon's pants, which was where her drink inevitably ended up. I stopped short. Gia swiped a few napkins from the table he stood by and fell to her knees. She furiously wiped at the front of his pants while words spilled from her lips.

"I'm so sorry," Gia babbled, her voice too sugary.

My mouth fell open, and my gut clenched.

"Let me just… help you fix the situation."

Is she serious? My gaze jumped from Gia to Damon, and my fists clenched at my sides.

Silence blanketed the space around us. People stared. They lifted their phones, and I reacted. Lunging forward, I yanked her to her feet, dragging her back. Her gaze jerked to the girls near Damon, who laughed, aiming their phones at her face.

"I-I…" Gia's wide, panic-stricken eyes locked onto my determined ones.

"Fuck them," I growled. "They're a bunch of assholes."

Tears welled in her eyes, and my heart broke for her.

"Go," I whispered so only she could hear me. I needed to stay and take care of something before I followed her.

I released her, and Gia fled toward the gate then to the beach. I stayed rooted to the spot, anger sizzling in my soul. *How fucking dare them.*

"Seems like your friend did everything she could to get me to fuck her. I bet she would have sucked me off right here if I wanted her to." Damon shrugged, the poster of indifference. "Too bad she's so easily scared off." He cocked his head, studying me too intently. "But not you."

I stepped closer to my target. The girls weren't worth my while. A smirk curved his sinful lips, and he mirrored my movement, bringing with him the spicy and sinful scent of his cologne along with that large, muscular body that made it difficult to breathe. I lingered a few seconds too long, distracted by his sheer size and athleticism.

"Did you want to finish the job your friend started? For you, I'm willing to find somewhere quiet inside."

My cheeks flamed. "Learn how to treat people, dickhead, or I'll kick your ass." I jerked away from him and whirled around.

Completely embarrassed and flustered, I had to shove through people to get to the gate. He was an asshole and always would be. But holy shit, did he smell good.

CHAPTER FOUR

DAMON

#Who'sThatGirl

I stood frozen in the same spot on my cousin's patio by the pool, visually following Sky as she stormed out after the incident with her band friend. Damn, I liked her walk.

Sky was the kind of girl who thought she was too good for me, her ideals too high, but I would show her. She would learn her place at our school.

Since our conversation after practice by the bleachers, I hadn't stopped thinking about her. And when Nicole, one of the cheerleaders hanging around after practice, had invited me to do whatever the fuck I wanted to her if we went inside, I hadn't. Usually, a first-day fuck helped me slide into a good school year. But all I could think about was Skylar.

"She's pretty feisty." Phoenix chuckled as he dropped into the space beside me. "When she threatened to kick your ass, I bought it."

"I'd like to see her try."

Phoenix punched my arm. "I just developed a theory, seeing as you're pretty fixated on that girl."

I tore my gaze from where Sky had gone and leveled it at my cousin. "What?"

"It feels like karma. The parties Shane and I throw are the Savages' epic downfalls."

"What are you talking about?" I didn't like where he was headed.

He leaned closer, whispering conspiratorially. "Riley… now Sky?"

"Fuck you." I shoved him away. "Just because Cole met Riley at one of your parties doesn't mean I'll end up with Sky McCormick." Though, I wouldn't mind her under me for a while.

I twitched my head in Shane's direction, where he was making out with Tracey in the pool.

"How's that going?"

Shane was the only one who'd committed to one girl besides my brother and Riley.

"The devil's own?" Phoenix growled. "It's still going strong. Shane's blind where she's concerned."

"He'll wake up eventually."

Tracey was opportunistic as hell. When Shane had shown interest in her two years ago, she'd locked that down hard because everyone knew our paths would lead to the NFL. No one else in the school showed promise to become a professional athlete. And everyone knew Tracey wanted that type of life. Why Shane couldn't see it was a mystery to all of us.

"I don't know," Phoenix said skeptically. "He might need divine intervention or something to get his head out of his ass."

"Or his dick out of her magical pussy."

Phoenix snorted. "Or that."

"So, how do you know Sky?" I gave up trying not to ask. The chick was permanently fixated in my mind.

"Lit class. She took an F on a major paper because she refused to read the *Scarlet Letter*. Said it demeans women."

"Huh."

"She could've just watched the movie. Demi Moore rocked that role."

He kept talking, and I pretended to listen. It was bad enough that I'd asked about her. And I wanted to know more but needed to find a way without coming across so thirsty.

CHAPTER FIVE

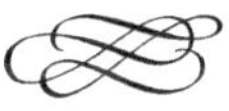

SKYLAR

#HunkyHSMan-ho

I finally got Gia to calm down after the nightmare at the Bennetts' barbeque bash with Damon Savage. Her face was splotchy and swollen, but she'd stopped hiccup talking, so that was progress. We huddled in her tree house, something we hadn't done for a very long time, and I wondered how it could still hold us. It wasn't far off the ground, but I worried. Since Gia was older, her dad hadn't kept up with whatever needed to be done to the wood to maintain it.

"Let's go back into the house. I feel like a giant." I shifted carefully. "And I weigh too much for this place to support me safely. It could come crashing down at any second with us in it. Not good."

Gia snorted. "Please, you're like half my size."

I frowned. She had a terrible body image, which was completely unreasonable. I wanted to beat the shit out of anyone who'd contributed to her low self-esteem. She had curves and was a little on the bigger side, but she was a knockout, in my opinion. Screw the skinny, I-starve-myself look. It didn't do anyone any good.

"Stop pointing out how small my boobs and butt are. You're giving me a boy-body complex."

"You know that's not what I meant." Gia rolled her red-rimmed eyes. "I would kill to look like you."

"Homeless?" I mimicked her and rolled my eyes. "Come on, seriously. I'm freaking out here, and I think I smell your mom cooking sauce. I'm starving."

Her family was Italian, and they *ate*. It was the best thing ever because they had me over regularly. Our fridge and pantry supply was meager at best. Mom did what she could and made sure I had food, but I was careful to leave plenty for her. She had the world on her shoulders as a hairdresser trying to pay all our bills.

We had several things going for us, though. Gia's family fed me more often than not, and I brought home leftovers because her mom insisted. Which meant my mom also had extra food. She needed it—she worked herself to the bone. Another plus was that I'd gotten a scholarship to Hidden Valley Academy when my middle school counselor had suggested I apply. It had required an essay, which had been a piece of cake for me. My counselor had helped push my application through, so I got to go to HVA for free—and received a meal card. A third plus was that the school didn't require uniforms. That was a real bonus because those could be expensive.

"Fine. Let's go. I'm hungry too." Gia gestured for me to climb down first, which I gladly did.

The tree house creeped me out. I swore I could still see the bloodstains in the corner where I'd huddled as a small child, hiding from my abusive dad. I shivered then shook off the bad memory, determined to put it firmly in the past, where it belonged. My feet touched the ground, and I breathed a sigh of relief, moving aside as Gia climbed down.

"Have you heard any more about your dad's parole?" She must have felt the misery and salvation clinging to the tree house's walls too.

I shuddered. "No."

The subject was too shitty to think about, and when I didn't say anything else, Gia dropped it.

Once inside the kitchen, the fantastic smells almost brought me to my knees. I had to check for drool at the corner of my mouth. I hadn't eaten breakfast, which was on me. Mom had gone shopping late last night after work, something she insisted on doing even when I offered to help.

Gia's mom, Gabriella, stood at the stove, stirring the sauce, and I couldn't resist drifting over.

"It smells amazing."

She patted my cheek, and a big smile spread across her face. "This is for dinner. We're having creamy tortellini soup. You girls can help yourself to the leftover ribs and antipasti for a snack."

"Can't wait." My mouth watered, and I hugged Gabriella, my second mom, before following Gia to her room.

Once back in Gia's room, I dropped into her desk chair, and she flopped onto her lavender bedspread. A canopy covered her bed with white gauzy ruffles tied back to the posts. The dreamy decor perhaps seemed a little young, but it fit Gia and her family, so I loved it.

I heard a sniffle, and my gaze jumped to my friend. Big crocodile tears rolled down her face. I braced myself. I loved Gia, but she was drama all the time.

"I'm humiliated!" she wailed. "I'll never be able to go back to school and face anyone."

She wasn't wrong. "Damon Savage is nothing more than a dumb jock with an overinflated ego."

"No, Sky." She didn't want to hear my thoughts. "He's a good guy in an impossibly horrible situation. You know what he went through when his mom committed suicide. It messed him up. He changed."

We both knew the story, but it looked like I would hear it again. I twisted my hair into a knot on top of my head and leaned back in my chair while she created a potential white knight from what was actually a demon—which was literally his nickname in the Ring.

"Give him a break. It must've been so hard for him to lose his mom like that—suicide—as he and Cole delivered the note to their dad. You should know better than anyone." Her gaze was hesitant, full of sympathy. "When stuff like that happens, it either kills you or makes you stronger. Look at you. You're the strongest person I know."

I gritted my teeth to stop the pain from doubling me over. I wasn't strong. I was scared shitless about what the future held for Mom and me with my dad's parole looming over us.

Gia pursed her full lips then sat cross-legged on her bed. I braced for the return of upbeat drama. It was better than the weepy shit any day.

"Do I need to remind you of the plan?" She pointed to the closet door, which remained securely shut. If her dad caught sight of that, heads would roll. "The plan does work with Damon. And I know you think this is stupid, but when I'm older, I don't want to look back on these days and wish I'd been different, taken the chance you keep trying to talk me out of."

"Gia—"

"No, Sky. Just listen. If I get laughed at, if the mean bitches end up teasing me until I want to run away, good news! I'm off to Notre Dame next year, and I won't be anywhere near them at Thane University to hear about it."

I mulled that over. It was a good point, and the best friend card was big for Gia. "Fine. But I think you can do better than hunky high school manwhore Damon."

Triumph flashed in Gia's dark eyes, and her cheeks flushed pink with excitement. There was no stopping the train wreck, so I might as well hop aboard.

"Damon is gorgeous. And that body!" She flopped back on the bed. "I think he has muscles on top of muscles. I can't wait to feel what it's like to be with him."

I tuned most of the Damon fan clubbing out. Still, I couldn't help but agree with most of it. Visually, he was the stuff of dreams. I hated myself for thinking anything sexual about the guy Gia had set her sights on. But thankfully, when he opened his mouth, the image shattered. Dominant, alpha asshole. That was who he was and the last thing I would ever want.

I got up to use her attached bathroom—she was seriously lucky with that. Mom and I shared one. With a flick of the switch, the room flooded with light, and I sucked in my breath. *No... Gia. Such a bad idea.* I grabbed the box of hair dye and stormed back into her room. "Please tell me you're not doing this. It's platinum blond." Gia was a dark brunette. "It'll destroy your hair."

She pushed herself up onto her elbows. "I'm not going to do it."

I narrowed my eyes. She'd answered too quickly. "It will turn out very bad. I'm begging you not to."

She rolled her eyes, heaved herself off the bed, then took the box from me and tossed it on her desk. "Let's get some food."

I pushed out a breath, went back into her bathroom, did what I needed to, and joined her in the hallway. My stomach was trying to eat itself. That was the only reason I let her get away without another lecture about what would happen if she used that dye. And I should know. Mom had told me horror stories about people coming to her to fix something stupid that they had done to their hair at home.

After satisfying my hunger with ribs and antipasti, I went home, promising Gabriella that I would return for dinner. She had mom's work schedule and always made sure I was at their dinner table when Mom had to work late.

They had bonded like sisters after what had happened with my dad. Gia's dad was protective of Mom too. They were like the older siblings she'd never had, and she adored them. I did too.

In my empty house, thoughts of everything that'd happened at the party, Gia gushing over Damon, and the way he'd smelled when he'd stepped close to me before I'd told him off circled in my head so much that I did something I never should have. I pulled him up on Insta. I got lost scrolling through his pictures. He was so hot, and it affected me in a way I wasn't proud of.

I paused on one of him in the Ring, no shirt, and every muscle deliciously defined. He was midpunch. The sheer focus and drive on his chiseled face made me want to reach into the picture and trace the hard angles of his jaw, maybe press a soft kiss to his lips. The contrast to the image I had of him in my mind was intense.

When I moved my thumb to scroll through more, my heart stopped. A red heart appeared on the picture—*from me.* I did that. I dropped my phone like it was lava. Jumping off the couch, I backed away like it was a bomb. The antipasti threatened to come back up. Freaking out, I paced our small living room. *He's got a shitload of followers. He's not going to notice one like.* He probably has a thousand notifications—nothing to worry about.

I would stick with that story.

CHAPTER SIX

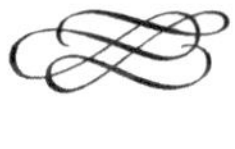

DAMON

#SneakAttack

Hidden Valley Academy Eagle Eye Blog

Potential Upset on the Horizon?
by Sky McCormick

Yesterday's last preseason practice for Hidden Valley Academy's unde-feated, national championship football team forecasts trouble. All-American receiving tight end Cole Savage was a vital loss to the team, and it appears they are struggling to stem the hemorrhage cause by his move to Thane University. Based on the final preseason practice, one might worry that Damon Savage can't follow in his older brother's footsteps.

HVA's quarterback, Phoenix Bennett, thrives under pressure and exceeds expectations with one accurate throw after another during yesterday's scrimmage. The connection to running back Shane Bennett promises points on the board as he blows through tackles and runs each catch into the end zone. Second-string tight end, Brennan Montgomery, warms up to his new starting position with solid tackles and two caught passes resulting in a gain of twenty-plus yards. It was when Phoenix tried to connect with running back Damon Savage that fumbles and lost yards occurred.

No comment from Damon Savage—or words this reporter can share.

Head Coach Tim Harris said, "We're missing one of our best players. His absence will be an adjustment."

When questioned about Damon, Harris said, "Cole's absence affects Damon and the rest of the team. Everyone has an off day, and the few botched plays today were no exception. But Damon's, Phoenix's, and Shane's sheer talent on the field will carry us through any adjustments we need to make. I expect great things from the team this year."

Time will tell if HVA's acclaimed football team will go on to repeat another undefeated year or suffer the first upsets the academy has seen in four years.

With an aggressive swipe, I closed the school's blog off my phone's screen. I had warned Sky at practice the other day that if she printed anything about me, she would pay for it. And I would keep my promise.

Today was a joke. Half days always were. Why the school thought it would be a good idea for the first day testified to the teachers wanting to be back as little as the students. It was second hour, and when Sky walked in and sat on the left side of the room next to some girl, I couldn't believe my luck.

All I had to do was wait for the bell to ring. She shifted in her seat but didn't turn around. *That's right. You're in my sights.* She probably sensed I'd zeroed in on her and the urge to run itched over her skin in an overwhelming fight-or-flight response.

Our teacher droned on about whatever the syllabus already listed for the first semester. Sunlight streamed through the windows on Sky's side of the room. I sat in the back next to Brad, who was on the team with me and seemed just as bored with the lecture as I felt, with his head forward, arms folded on his chest, and eyes closed.

A glance at the clock showed we had five more minutes of nothing before class ended. Neither Brad nor I had brought anything, and the black tabletop remained empty as his quiet snores rumbled beside me.

Seconds ticked by like a stopwatch before the signal gun fired for a sprint. I was up and closing in on Sky as soon as the bell rang. I let her get out the door and into the hall before I wrapped my hand around her arm and pulled her aside, pushing her back against the lockers as I crowded her.

Anger rippled over me, along with my ever-present attraction when she was near. Stormy-blue eyes met mine as she jerked her arm away. I released her but remained in her space.

"That was a foolish move."

"You'll have to be more specific." Sarcasm dripped off her words.

"The blog article."

A slow, wicked smile curved her full lips. "I write the truth."

I wanted to do so many things to her, but it wasn't the place or time. Still, I flattened one hand on the locker beside her head, sliding my other hand up her arm until my palm rested around the base of her throat. I applied subtle pressure, enjoying the way her pulse beat erratically.

"That wasn't the truth, and we both know it." I eyed her lips like a starving man. I wanted a taste. "I know my talent on the field, and now"—I eased my hand back, so my thumb brushed over her pounding pulse at the base of her neck—"I have my answer of what, or who, rather, you want." I released her and backed away, not once taking my eyes off her.

She crossed her arms over her chest and glared. "You're just as delusional off the field as on it."

I laughed. I had no illusions about football. I was damn good at what I did. "I meant what I said that day. You'll have hell to pay for what you did, and I will collect one way or another."

Sky could act like she wasn't into me, and I had no doubt she didn't like me, but her body's reaction said otherwise. I planned to enjoy my revenge.

That mouth would be mine.

Skylar

"What the fuck is this?" Stephanie slapped a printed screenshot on the desk before me that I'd written for the day's blog post. She leaned over me, her palms flat on the table, fury darkening her face until she turned an unflattering shade of red. The small scar above her eyebrow stood out like a beacon.

She'd called an emergency editorial meeting. The rest of the team who had gathered in the classroom was oddly quiet.

"It's the article you assigned me." I held back a grin. My sarcasm only made her angrier.

"Explain yourself." Her clipped words punctuated her frustration as she pushed away and paced before me.

I remained seated as if I'd been called to task in the principal's office. I guess, in a way, I had. *Is her hair getting curlier?* Sometimes, I swore her corkscrew curls took on a life of their own.

Fine. I gave in. "If it was such an issue, why didn't you flag it before it went to print?"

"I trusted you to do your job."

"And I did. Damon had a shit game. I reported it." *For fuck's sake.* "It's not my fault you didn't do your job and read it before you let the page go live."

Stephanie's eyes closed, and I imagined she was counting to ten before she spoke. I counted along with her.

"I got a call from the athletics director."

Yep, she'd counted to ten. I shrugged. "And?"

"He was furious, and he demanded a retraction."

I snorted. "That's crazy. I reported facts. And Damon played terribly."

Her narrowed eyes bore into me. "I took the article down."

My hands flattened on the desk, and I pushed myself up, leaning forward, inches from her face. "One teacher complains, and you bend over and take it? I thought you wanted an honest report of events."

Her arms crossed over her chest. The rest of the people in the room observed us like it was a tennis match. Ball was in her court, and they looked to her for a rebuttal. I wanted to hear it too.

"Players have an off day, Sky. Your article showcased him as a joke. A star player, mind you."

I clenched my jaw to stop myself from saying more. That was ridiculous.

"Whether you like him or not"—she looked to the ceiling for a moment—"he brings in scouts. Do you honestly want to blow that for the other players who could get noticed because of the hype around Damon, Phoenix, or Shane?"

I hated that she made sense. I still disagreed with her, but I did understand her point. None of that changed that I was boiling mad she had taken my article down.

"You don't bash one of the Elite." The color ebbed from her face as panic tinged her voice. She was worked up over it, and not just about the athletic director calling her.

Huh. "Are you scared of them?"

"Like you're not."

"I'm not." It was a partial truth. I feared how Damon made me feel. It wasn't always hate between us. Sometimes, it felt like pure, undeniable lust.

CHAPTER SEVEN

DAMON

#Miscreant

Of all the days I had to come down early before school... The last thing I wanted was a conversation with my dad's wife.

"Good morning." Raelyn leaned a hip against the counter, holding a steaming cup of coffee. "Do you want some breakfast?"

"No." *Am I an asshole?* Sure, but I hadn't asked for my situation.

"Damon." Dad's voice boomed through the kitchen as he entered behind me. "Try again."

Anger licked up my spine, and I narrowed my gaze. "Thanks, Raelyn, but no."

"Have a great day today, Damon." Pink colored her cheeks, and she eased away from the island to the kitchen table, where she smiled at my dad. I knew what she was doing, trying to defuse the situation by getting him to focus away from me and on where she'd moved.

It wouldn't work, and my skin prickled from his proximity as he followed me into the garage. Once the door shut, I turned to face him. Eye to eye, we both stood a few inches over six feet, which annoyed me. His jaw clenched. Power and focused intensity crackled around him, and I knew he had put his lawyer hat on for our conversation.

"What?" I had to poke him.

I didn't know why I couldn't accept what I'd learned about him and let it go, as Cole had over time. Well, I did know. Finding out my idol had cheated on my mom with Raelyn, who he'd married after Mom had taken her life, was a total mindfuck.

He shook his head, disappointment as clear as day in his green eyes, similar to Cole's. "You can stop the pissed-off-at-the-world attitude and grow up. Raelyn has done nothing to you and doesn't deserve how you treat her."

"Except she's the other woman." I was so close to my car. I just wanted to get in and drive away. Everything about him pissed me off.

"Stop blaming her for something that wasn't her fault."

"What are you talking about? Mom's death? Or that you're a cheater? Hell, she is, too, since she knew you were married."

"Enough. I won't tolerate your behavior any longer. You're smarter than this. Taking out your anger for me on Raelyn is wrong." A hard gleam entered his eyes. "How do you think Riley would feel knowing you're treating her mom poorly?"

Yeah, that wasn't going to work. "She would understand. She wasn't all that happy with the two of you either."

"Before she knew what we meant to one another."

Fucker. "Again, at the cost of Mom's life."

"I see myself in you more and more lately." He shook his

head. "The drive, but so much anger simmers beneath that. It's not good for you. Trust me. I know."

"The last thing I want is to be like you." It was my worst fucking nightmare. "To destroy my wife's world so the only option she sees is to kill herself? No thanks. I'm trying to do whatever I can not to be like you." I backed toward my SUV, avoiding the knowing look on his face.

"You're intelligent enough to know what really happened in our family. Especially after I sat down with you and Cole and told you everything."

"Whatever." I got it. I did. But that didn't mean I had to be okay with what had gone down or with how in the dark I'd been. Our conversation needed to end.

"Are you sure you want to go into the NFL? You would excel as a lawyer."

I snorted. Even if I did want that, I would never tell him. "I have school. I'll be nicer to Raelyn, but that's it. You and I aren't okay."

Dad said nothing. He just continued to watch me as I got into the SUV and backed out of the driveway, turning toward school. I blasted music to get him out of my head so I could face the first real day of school without the past taking up too much of my mind.

I stood outside the academy's front doors, leaning against the wrought iron railing, keeping an eye on the parking lot for when Skylar arrived. Her Instagram notification had popped up last night, and I hadn't been able to stop thinking about her since.

When her friend had dropped to her knees and tried to rub the wetness from her drink off my jeans, all I'd been able to picture was Sky there, her black hair fisted in my hand as I fed my cock past those fuck-me lips of hers.

Phoenix and Shane jogged over from the lot, slowing as they caught sight of me. Tracey latched onto Shane's arm then wound her arms around Shane's neck. They kissed, oblivious to where they were.

It gave Phoenix the opening he seemed to be waiting for. "How pissed are you?"

"Sky's article?" Fucking furious. "She and I'll have words later." I kept my voice even, not wanting to draw attention.

"Miller got it removed."

The athletic director. I figured. He dealt with all sports program issues, football especially, with an unhealthy intolerance for everything else. Not that I minded, but he could be a little zealous in his hovering. "The article doesn't matter. No one gives a shit."

Phoenix shrugged. "No. It doesn't."

He dropped it as Tracey and Shane came up for air, and I continued to watch for Sky's arrival.

Then Phoenix knocked my shoulder with his. "Come on. We can't be late for class on our first full day." Yesterday's half day didn't count in any of our minds. "And Coach wants to meet with the three of us this week. We need time to set that up before the bell."

Having only the three of us at the academy felt strange, and I missed the hell out of my brother, Cole. But he was already making a name on the football field at Thane. My cousins and I would go there, too, when we graduated.

And since Cole was gone, Phoenix kept Shane and me in line with workouts and practice-related stuff. Cole and Phoenix were the most driven about making it into the NFL. I was down for it but would consider it no big deal if I didn't get picked up. I had other tentative plans for a career. I just wasn't sure about my major yet. But I had time.

I paused at Phoenix's locker in the main hallway, needing to see Sky like my next fix. Something about that girl tempted me irrationally. Then she walked in with those incredible lips, dark hair flowing behind her shoulders and a face that had starred in my dreams last night. Her body was slender and would fit perfectly under my arm. I wanted her more than I could comfortably admit.

I eased away from my cousins and Tracey to intercept Sky with a hand on her arm. I pulled her aside, and all the wicked thoughts I'd had last night roared to the surface. "Did you ditch your friend to be alone with me? Because I'm down for that. I have my brother's key to the school basement." I had no doubt that she knew we sparred down there after school hours, when the basement would be locked, and most importantly, where we were away from my dad's prying eyes. "We can get hot and sweaty without anyone knowing."

She yawned, and I clenched my teeth, annoyed by her bored reaction. It wasn't something I got from chicks. Ever. I studied her for signs that she was full of shit. When I spotted the pulse in her throat, not just beating but pounding, a rush of satisfaction flooded me and eased the ache forming at my jaw. I knew she was into me. Her reaction had been a hundred percent in response to how close we were and the things I'd said to her.

"Where are your miscreant friends?" Her pretty blue eyes widened. "I'm sorry. I shouldn't have used such a big word. It means good-for-nothing, very bad, even evil."

And the ache was back as a muscle jumped along the side of my jaw. I hated being called stupid. I was third in our fucking class. I was about to tell her that when her friend walked into the school with pumpkin-orange hair.

Sky followed my line of sight and sucked in a breath. Then she took off, grabbing her friend's arm and dragging her into the nearest girl's bathroom. The sight was shocking, but I didn't laugh. Her friend had fucked up, whatever. It wasn't anything I cared about or needed to belittle.

But the others in the hall didn't seem to think that with all their laughter. I seriously doubted Sky would be out anytime soon, so I turned back to my cousins. Jessica, one of the cheerleaders and my sometimes go-to girl to mess around with, latched onto my arm, her smile wide with laughter.

"Did you get a load of pumpkin head?" Jessica asked.

Tracey was the only one who cared. The two girls gossiped while Phoenix caught my eye then rolled his.

"She was a band-geek freak of no notice before." Tracey smirked.

I caught Phoenix's glare—his absolute hatred for his brother's girlfriend.

"And it looks like she's aiming her sights higher"—Tracey and Jessica looked pointedly at me—"where she doesn't belong."

From the corner of my eye, a flash of orange caught my notice. Sky and her friend came out of the bathroom. Jessica and Tracey still snickered, saying some bullshit none of us cared about. Sky paused and shot my group a glare, then walked out with her friend.

Excitement coursed through me at her fiery strength. The year had just gotten a hell of a lot more interesting.

CHAPTER EIGHT

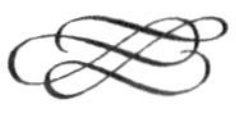

SKYLAR

#CounterOffer

With the academy in my rearview mirror, I sped away with Gia bawling in the passenger seat of my tiny black Fiat that used to be Mom's. No one was home at my place, so we headed there. Mom was at work, and we had no old man to worry about because my dad was in prison for beating Mom almost to death. He was supposed to be out soon, which created a constant worry at the back of my mind.

But right then, I had to deal with Gia's hair-tastrophe. "What the hell happened? I thought you weren't going to go all 'beauty school dropout' and try to dye your hair." I turned down our street, bypassed her house, and pulled into my driveway. After hurrying her out of the car, I took her into the house.

By that time, she'd gotten more control over her spiraling emotions, meaning the tears had stopped, which was helpful. I got her seated at the kitchen table and set a glass of water in front of her. Holding up my finger, I pressed the button on my phone to call Mom. She answered just before I thought it might go to voicemail, and I sagged against the chair.

"Mom, Gia messed up her hair trying to dye it blond. Is there any way you can fit her in today?"

"What was she thinking?" Mom groaned. "Never mind. I don't have time to hear it. I'm at the end of a cut and color. But I have a break in an hour and, lucky for you two, a cancellation before that. Be here at the salon in fifteen."

I thanked her for both of us then hung up. "Mom's going to fix it."

Gia's lip quivered. "I know I shouldn't have done it. But the box was calling out to me. I wanted to be a blonde."

"This is getting out of control." Her drive to accomplish the things on her senior goals list would end miserably if I didn't do something to help. And I didn't just mean getting Mom to fix her hair.

"I knew I shouldn't have done it when my head started stinging then burning. And now Damon has seen me looking like I dipped my head in a vat of pumpkin spice." She buried her face in her hands, her words and sheer misery muffled. "I thought the plan would work better and I would have had more fun if I were blond and could snag his attention."

"Well, you've gotten his attention twice now."

Gia's head whipped up, and she glared. "Not helping."

"You're being dramatic. It isn't that bad." It was. I knew how Damon and his crew were. They were assholes who pounced.

"It isn't that bad?" She stood, her hands flying around, as she liked to talk with them. "I've ruined everything. I might as well give up and crawl into my bathtub and hide until graduation."

"It's going to be okay. I promise. And if anyone teases you or says anything, I'll pummel, pound, or annihilate them." Not that I'd ever hit anyone before, but I had a reputation for being a badass since I'd yelled at Portia Mulligan and threatened to shove her head in the toilet in fifth grade for calling Gia an Italian sausage.

Gia gave a watery smile, and I grabbed her hand, pulling her back outside to my car.

"We need to go. Mom's probably about ready for you."

Mom worked at a salon in town, where she rented a chair that she said cost so much because of where the salon was located—right on Main Street. It was a good thing she was so talented because that meant she had plenty of clients. I parked, and Gia and I walked in with a wave to Tiffany at the front desk. Everyone knew who I was because I looked just like Mom, just a younger version. We were even the same five-foot-six height.

Mom turned and then lifted some of Gia's hair. "Oh, honey. What did you do?"

More tears welled in Gia's eyes, and Mom patted her arm.

"Have a seat. This is fixable." She met my eyes in the mirror over Gia's head. "Sky, you need to get back to school. I'll call Gabi to come get Gia when we're done."

"Thanks, Mom." I smiled then rushed out. If I hurried, I would make it in time for chemistry—one of the classes I happened to have with Damon.

I raced back to the academy, shocked that I didn't get a ticket. Luck was probably on my side for that. Unfortunately, it might not be much longer. I planned to tempt fate with a proposition for Damon. Because the shit with Gia needed to stop. She was putting herself in too many compromising situations, and I didn't want her epic senior year to turn into a monstrous nightmare that made her cringe every time she remembered it. That wasn't what she had in mind, and I might have a way to fix it.

In the halls, I grabbed my Chem book then headed to class as the bell rang. The hallways flooded with people, but I only needed to find one.

Shrill laughter skated unpleasantly along my spine, raising the hairs on the back of my neck as Jessica, Damon's usual arm candy slammed her locker. Tracey and Eve, friends of hers, fell into step beside her as she pushed away from her locker. Our eyes met, and an evil glint eclipsed hers.

"Did you see the thirsty fool with the carrot dye job slobbering around Damon?" Jessica's smile turned downright evil. "We're gonna have some fun with her."

"Puh-lease, was it possible not to miss?" Eve's high-pitched voice shrilled through the hallway chatter.

"It's hilarious." Tracey fluffed her blond hair. "Gotta run. See you two bitches at lunch."

"Later." Eve turned down the foreign language hallway, leaving Jessica too close but alone.

Anger rolled through me in dangerous waves, and I smirked at Jessica, stepping in front of her and forcing her to stop. "That's not gonna happen because I can mean girl you right back. Only"—dark intent swirled through me in a cauldron of pleasure—"it'll be in print, and the entire school will know about it."

Jessica's hand found her hip, and she glared with a confidence possessed only by the upper echelon in our stupid school. But she didn't fool me. My comment had found its mark, evident by the slight pallor to her skin.

Most girls might be intimidated by someone with the power and backing of the Elite, but I wasn't one of those. I didn't feel bad. She was a bully, and it was time someone put her in her place. And drive it home even more.

"Just think of all the unflattering pictures I could capture. Mistakes even. Things that could cost you a part of life you deem very important."

Her cloying perfume clogged the airspace between us as she leaned forward. "I would crush you if you tried to do anything so stupid. And not only me, but the Elite, and all of the squad associated with them."

I snorted. "You can try. But once they see what an unfavorable article does to you, do you really think they'll rush to your defense and risk one about them?" I scanned for a few of her people in the crowd. "I guess it's just a risk you'll have to take if you keep going after Gia."

Jessica flipped her hair over her shoulder. "You have no power." She skimmed me from head to toes. "You're nobody. The joke's on you. I can do whatever I want, and you can't touch me. Something you should know after trying to do the same thing with that bogus article about Damon. Nothing you said diminished how he's perceived. And it'll be the same for me."

I grinned wide. "Big difference is that you're not one of the Elite. You're not untouchable." Done with the conversation, I pushed past her so she could stew on the truth I'd dropped on her.

It was no skin off my back if she chose to ignore me and continued to go after my best friend. She would learn real quick who her real friends were after I published something unflattering on her, and my guess was that very few would remain by her side.

I took the stairs nearest the science wing then hurried to the door, shedding the bad taste in my mouth from talking to Jessica. I had another issue to take care of that might not be as easy to fix. I didn't think Damon would be there early, but I wanted to try talking to him before the teacher started class.

As tingles raced over my arms and up the back of my neck, I knew who had entered without looking. When I sensed him draw near, I stood from my seat and latched onto his arm, tugging him over to the large bank of windows. He let me lead him there. I wasn't foolish enough to think I could physically move the guy. But that was good. It meant he would at least hear me out.

"How's Polly Pumpkin Head?"

Fucker. I sucked in a deep breath and let it out slowly. Our eyes met and held, and I hardened myself to the fireworks exploding inside my body at his nearness.

"I want to make a deal with you." I kept my voice low so no one could overhear what I was about to say. It was one of those spur-of-the-moment things that I had no plan to back up but that escaped my mouth before I could stop it. "I'll do your homework in all your classes for as long as you date Gia."

My heart thundered against my rib cage so hard I thought it would crack. Beads of sweat formed along my hairline. I felt wild and out of control, not my usual self. A sexy, devious smirk slowly tugged at his lips, and I found myself holding my breath.

"I have a counteroffer," he said.

But then the teacher called the class to order. The glimmer in his eye made something tingle in my stomach as we broke apart to take our seats. The scary thing was, I planned to listen to his terms.

CHAPTER NINE

DAMON

\#Symbiosis

Chemistry was the longest hour of my life. Just thinking about Sky, being in the same room with her made me hot and hard. I willed the clock to go faster. We had things to discuss.

I had a great view of Sky from the back of the classroom. Her dark hair fell down her back in thick waves, almost to her narrow waist. She had a fantastic ass, not too big or small. I wanted her, and nothing I did had convinced me I could walk away without a taste.

I wasn't someone who had to blackmail or bribe anyone. At HVA, I was a fucking god and could have any girl I set my sights on. Except for Sky, who couldn't move her stool farther from the aisle—creating more distance between us—and from my sight.

Letting her slip out with most of the class when the bell finally rang, I hung back so no one would be listening behind me when we spoke. I licked my lips as I exited the classroom, hungering to feel her mouth on me, to feel her softness. I didn't even mind her acerbic tongue. In truth, I liked it. She had a backbone of steel and fire that burned hot in the blue depths of her eyes. I looked forward to every moment she would bend to my will, something I knew wasn't in her nature.

Across from the classroom, she leaned a hip against a bank of lockers. I liked to see her waiting for me. I matched her pose, standing closer than I thought she would be comfortable with. And I couldn't wait for her reaction to what I was about to propose.

"Name your price." Her voice was raspy and sexy as hell.

"Meet me in the basement at lunch."

Her eyes widened. "No."

I grinned, enjoying this way more than I thought I would. "Then, I guess you don't need anything from me, so..." I straightened to leave.

"Life is full of disappointments." She delivered her hushed words like a whip. "My friend will get over it."

Shit, she would walk. I grabbed her arm, and she glared at my hand until I released her.

"Just meet me in the basement at lunch, and we can work out the details. No fooling around. I won't lay a hand on you." *Not one that you don't ask me to put on you, anyway.*

The morning dragged, but when I got to the basement, she was there, her fingers laced in front of her. From how tightly she squeezed them, the color had drained, the only giveaway to her discomfort. If I hadn't caught that, I would have thought she seemed bored, from the disinterested expression she wore with ease.

"What are the mats about?" She scrunched her nose. "Will I need to disinfect my shoes after this?"

I worked to suppress a smile. She was amusing. "No. It's where my cousins and I come to spar for the fights."

"Those fights are stupid. You'll get caught one day, and where will that leave you? With a record?" Her brows rose in challenge. "Or in jail?"

Any other girl would have been impressed. Skylar was a mystery I wanted to spend time figuring out. She intrigued me. I waited to see what else came out of that sarcastic little mouth of hers. I knew I wouldn't have to wait long and that she wouldn't disappoint.

"What are your demands? Hurry up so I can go take an acid bath."

I held still, analyzing everything about her. The more uncomfortable or angry she felt, the more caustic she became. I'd pushed her enough, and I wanted to find out how far she would go to help her friend.

"I'll date your friend, but you have to make it up to me."

"How do you expect me to 'make it up' to you?"

I moved closer, my fingers itching to touch her. "I'll lose out on a lot of ass if everyone thinks I'm dating Gia exclusively."

Sky shook her head, her dark hair tumbling around her shoulders and her blue eyes practically glowing with hatred. "You're an asshole." She moved to leave.

I couldn't let her. My fingers wrapped around her arm, and I pulled her back. "I'm going to kiss you, then you can decide if the payback is fair."

Her body tensed, and I knew she would be unwilling if I pulled her closer. So I moved in and slid my hand in a slow caress from her wrist to the back of her neck. I kept my touch light, enjoying the softness of her skin as if we had all day and not just a few more minutes of our lunch period. My other hand rested on her hip as I lowered my mouth to hers.

I brushed her lips in a soft caress then grazed her bottom lip with my teeth before tracing the seam with my tongue. She gasped, and my mouth slanted over hers. When her hands wound around my neck, I pulled her closer, angling her head to deepen the kiss. I took my time exploring. She tasted as amazing as I had instinctively known she would.

I was lost in the way she felt in my arms, the way she responded. She was fucking incredible and kissed like she was born to do it. By the time I ended the kiss, I was so hard I wasn't sure I could walk up the stairs.

Centimeters separated us, our breaths coming fast and out of control. I needed to shake the thrall she had over me and would do it through the terms to seal the deal she seemed so invested in for her friend.

"I date your friend, and you're grateful." Time ticked loudly in my ears as I waited for her to answer.

Then the familiar anger I associated with her flared brightly. She needed another push, and I was more than willing to give it to her.

I dropped my hands and stepped back. "Forget it."

"Fine," she snapped.

The attraction between us blazed hot. I couldn't wait to have her in my arms again, especially when she was agitated and feisty. It made things more than interesting.

"But your dates with Gia have to be *real* dates, and everybody has to believe that you're together, so you can't be driving her down the coast and hiding her. And you can't tell anyone about our deal. Especially Gia or any of your stupid friends. You have to act like Gia is your girl."

"Fine." I kept a tight rein on my emotions. I was so close to getting her under me, and I wouldn't screw it up by letting her know how annoyed I was about the friend. "But you're going to have to make up for all the action I won't be getting."

I would need her far more than she thought. The only other outlet I had to burn energy was football and fighting. Sex was a huge relief, and I didn't know how long I could go without all three before I lost my mind. Without Cole around, I had no buffer between dad and me.

Her lips pressed tight, and she nodded. Fuck no, that wasn't going to work. "I need the words, Skylar." My voice was dark and dangerous, giving her a peek at what she would be getting into.

"Fine." The corner of her lips lifted in a closed-mouth smile, making me think of a cat that had just eaten the family bird. "Gia wants to be prom queen."

Is she delusional? "I'm not a fucking magician. How am I supposed to make a nobody into a prom queen?"

One slim shoulder lifted in a shrug. "If you can't do it, then forget it. That's the deal."

"Prom queen is extra," I growled, envisioning everything I would do to Sky for payback.

"If you can make it happen, you can ask for whatever you want."

Oh, I will. I definitely will.

CHAPTER TEN

SKYLAR

#WoW

Shivers raced over my body. Holy hell, Damon could kiss. I stopped at the top landing to the ground floor, pressing my back against the cool wall. My fingers rested on my tingling lips. It was like I could still feel him there. The way he had eased me into the kiss was everything I'd ever dreamed about and nothing like I'd experienced before.

I hadn't wanted him to stop. When his hand had settled on my hip, guiding me where he wanted, my thoughts had gone out the window, and all I could do was feel. I was in a world of trouble because that kiss—it was memorable and magnificent. And I wanted more.

The bell rang to signal the end of our lunch period, and I walked down the hall, trembling as I relived over and over again what he'd done to me. He might actually be worth the hype, because that kiss continued to work through my blood.

I wandered the halls in a daze. Some part of my brain remembered my schedule, and I found myself seated in physics. Not that being in the right place did me any favors. I existed in a fog and could almost understand why Jessica followed Damon around like an eager puppy.

More than once, when I should have been listening to a teacher or getting something from my locker, I found myself touching my lips, remembering. He knew what he was doing, and I hated to admit it, but I was dangerously intrigued.

Ugh. My kiss infatuation was with *Damon*—a dumb jock, someone I should hate on principle. I tossed my pen on my desk, ignoring the looks I got from the people around me. *What was I thinking making a deal like that?* It would be even worse if Gia fell for him and he stopped being just a means to an end.

Okay, that was a mean way to think of her objective with Damon. But if he got a taste of his own medicine—because he was definitely using me and was generally an ass—then all the better. Maybe he would think before he decided to use and lose a girl next time.

A body slammed against the locker next to mine as I put away a book. I glanced over, expecting it to be Damon—we would have words about him singling me out if it was him. I turned with a scowl already in place.

"Oh, wow. Gia…" I touched her platinum-blond hair that had been straightened and fell silkily around her face, ending just above her shoulders. "You look fabulous."

"Thanks." She vibrated with excitement. "He hasn't seen me yet."

"Well, when he does, he'll trip over himself because you look like a knockout. And… he'll be lucky to have you."

"I hope so." A self-deprecating huff pushed through her lips. "I need to erase the past."

She touched the shorter strands that Mom must have had to

cut off due to damage. Or wherever, it didn't matter. The cut was incredible on her. I had no idea she would look like that, and I bet Damon wouldn't either. A slow smile curved my lips. I couldn't wait to see his face. Maybe he would even forget about our deal and be into her. It could work.

"What did your mom think?"

Mine couldn't take her back to school because of my mom's job, and since Gia's mom worked from home, my mom had called hers.

Gia rolled her eyes then looped her arm through mine. We walked toward our next class, which, thank God, was our last one.

We sat next to each other, waiting for the final bell to sound. Several people stared. I couldn't blame them. She looked like a completely different person. And the confidence it gave her only added to her allure.

"She was furious. By some miracle, I had managed to sneak out for school before she saw me this morning. But when your mom called her"—she shook her head, eyes wide—"the entire car ride was in Italian."

We had to stop talking when the teacher started the class. And when we were finally released, I was relieved because, again, I hadn't heard a word my teacher had said. As we exited the classroom, it was to find Damon leaning against the lockers opposite our door. I had a moment of déjà vu from when I had done the same, waiting for him and to name his price, but I quickly shook *that* off.

His eyes glided over me, and I felt them like a sensual caress. I gripped my book tighter, willing his effects to go away. Then he spotted Gia, and if he was surprised, he didn't show it. A lazy grin spread across his mouth before he crooked his finger to her.

Asshole, what a dick move. I turned to snap for Gia not to respond to him, but she was gone. I forced myself to turn and walk to my locker when he touched her hair. I couldn't watch. It was what I wanted him to do, to ask her out, but I hated every minute of it. *Because he's a jerk, not because of how he affects me.*

I was shoving my books into my backpack when Gia ran up to me and squealed. *Fuck no.* I grabbed her hand and shushed her. People were looking, and I didn't want them to have another reason to give her a hard time.

"He asked me out." She did a happy little jig, and I couldn't help but laugh.

"Yeah? You think the hair did it?"

She touched the shorn strands and sighed. "Yeah. Your mom is a miracle worker."

"Please. She just did an emergency cut and color. Your face didn't change. You've always been beautiful. The only person who couldn't see that was you."

She rolled her eyes, but color stained her cheeks. "And the entire school. But whatever."

"So, when are you going out?" *And what does that mean for me?* Hopefully nothing. Because she was beautiful, and he would be lucky to have her attention.

"We're going out after football practice. I'm so excited I feel like I might throw up."

"Uh, gross?"

"Hey, I have a favor to ask you."

"Shoot." I nervously checked down the hallway, expecting to find Damon staking me.

"You know how strict my parents are."

Yep, no explanation needed there. But I kind of loved that about them. "Yeah."

"I'm going to tell them I'm at your place."

"Yeah, okay." I had figured I would have to cover.

Gia gushed about Damon all the way from the school until

we got into our cars. And that was when the guilt hit me hardest. It would kill Gia if she ever found out that Damon was only taking her out because I agreed to pay him in favors. *If he ever tells Gia, I'm going to kill him.*

50

CHAPTER ELEVEN

DAMON

#Payback

The date with Gia was fine, nothing much to it. Hungry from football practice, I took her out to get a burger and fries. I shoveled food in my mouth while she picked at hers, chatting a mile a minute. I think I grunted or said one or two noncommittal things. The chick obviously worshipped me, which usually made for some fun times getting laid. She was a pretty girl, genuine enough, but I wasn't into her. It was her friend who had my attention.

I couldn't wait to take Gia home. By the time I did, it was dark outside, which worked for what I had in mind. After I dropped her off, I sent Skylar a text saying I would pick her up. It was time to collect payment.

Sky: *I'm busy*

Yeah, that wasn't going to work for me.

Me: *Get unbusy*

Sky: *Not gonna happen*

I moved forward one house and parked. Sky and Gia lived next to each other—convenient.

Me: *I can come to the door. I'm parked out front*

Two seconds later, her front door opened, and she jogged down the walkway, yanked open my passenger door, and hopped inside. "Go."

I laughed at her flash of teeth and general pissy attitude. A park nearby offered enough privacy for what I wanted from her. The air felt charged between us, and her nearness affected me in ways I couldn't wait to explore. I turned into the parking lot and picked a spot not too far from a streetlight. I wanted to see her.

Awareness and expectation buzzed over my skin like the best kind of high. It had taken all my willpower to keep to the speed limit and maintain my destination rather than pulling up to the curb and yanking her over the console and into my lap. The taste of her lips still lingered on mine from earlier in the basement. The erotic fantasy had played in my head on repeat throughout the day. I couldn't wait to have all of her. I wanted to hear the sounds she made when I buried myself inside her.

Sky glanced at her phone then shot off a text. "Thanks for making the date with Gia a good one."

"Sure." My grin held every predatory thought rolling around in my mind. "Now you owe me. A hand job should do it." I parked and patted my Range Rover's console for her to hop onto on over.

"Are you fucking kidding me?" Her head jerked back, and she positioned herself against the door. Anger flashed in her eyes and dripped from her hostile expression. "A hand job? Are you twelve?"

"Good to know you've been giving out hand jobs since you were in elementary school."

"Gah." She gagged.

Damn, she amused me. "If I'd gone on a real date with a

chick of my choice, I would be getting a lot more than a hand job right now."

She crossed her arms over her chest. "Forget it."

"No problem." I called her bluff and started the car. She needed a little push because I was in no way done blackmailing her. "I'll just tell Gia I'm not interested."

"Fine. I'll do it," she snapped. "You know, I really hate you."

"You don't need to like me for this." I curled my hand around her arm and tugged her closer, then leaned in to kiss her lips because I couldn't stop fantasizing about them.

"Whoa." She jerked her arm free, a dangerous gleam in her eyes as she smirked. "What do you think you're doing? Hand jobs don't include making out."

I froze for a second, unsure of what I wanted. Kissing her was amazing, and I could probably be satisfied if that were all she was willing to do. But then, thinking about her hand around my dick made it so I could barely see straight.

I went with that one, as I'd kissed her earlier. It still wouldn't be enough. I wanted so much more from her. "Fine." I backed up and let her get to it.

A second or two passed, then her hands were on my belt, fumbling to release it. I brushed her hand away and did it myself. Seeing her do the rest would be better if my dick didn't punch its way through my zipper in its eagerness to get to her. "Unfasten my pants."

I watched, intrigued, as her hands shook and she struggled with the button. My pants were getting tighter. I wanted her to hurry up, but I also couldn't get enough of seeing that strong, sexy girl get nervous. She fascinated me to the point I wanted to experience everything I could with her, everything that she would let me.

The more she struggled, the tighter my pants got. If she didn't hurry, they would bust open. I popped the button, and as she worked the zipper, I slid my hand behind her neck and fisted her thick, silky hair. A slight pressure, and I had her face angled so I could kiss her.

Fuck the hand job. My mouth slanted over hers, and I groaned at her taste. I didn't think I would ever get enough. So soft, and she smelled amazing, like vanilla with a hint of coconut. I could easily do that for hours and be happy. *That has happened before... never.*

She stopped messing with my pants and kissed me back. I hauled her closer, or as much as I could with the restrictions of the front seat. The feel of her lips against mine erased my ever-present anger with my dad, how much I missed my brother, and the need to expend energy by fighting or fucking. Sky was the best goddammed balm to it all.

I sucked her lower lip into my mouth, and she melted against me as I toyed with her, exploring and coaxing every response I could from her. It was addictive. The breathy moans drove me mad.

When her hand wrapped around my dick, I almost came from the contact. I thrust into her palm and devoured her mouth greedily. With every stroke, I swelled impossibly more and had to fight to last. The pad of her thumb grazed over the tip, and I angled her head farther to deepen our kiss. *Who needs air?*

When she cupped my balls, stars formed behind my eyelids, then her hand glided up and down in slow sensual strokes with just the right amount of pressure. I couldn't take it anymore. I exploded all over her hand and myself.

That was insane and a little embarrassing. I haven't come that fast since I was in seventh grade, when Sara Jensen gave me my first blow job. But my time with Skylar was a hundred times better.

I'd never come so hard in my life, and I feared I might black out for a second or two. As soon as she finished me off, she tore her mouth from mine, breathing hard. At least I wasn't the only one affected by what we'd just done.

I kept my gaze locked on her flushed face, bright eyes, and deliciously swollen lips as I reached one-handed into the back seat and yanked some clothes from my workout bag on the floor. I handed her a shirt for her hands and cleaned myself up with a pair of shorts. When she was done, I took the shirt back and tossed both in the back.

After tucking myself in and zipping up, I started the car and took her home. Neither of us said a word. As I pulled up to the curb in front of her house, I leaned over to kiss her again. But she was out of the car and dashing up to her front door before I could.

A dark laugh filled the inside of my SUV. Skylar had proved to be a hell of a lot more entertaining than I ever could have imagined. And suddenly, I had a plan—I would take her friend out every night I could.

CHAPTER TWELVE

SKYLAR

#Regret

I *can't believe I jerked him off in the front seat of his SUV.* And at the park I played at when I was five until around twelve years old. I let myself into the house and leaned against the front door, needing a minute. The lights were on. *Did I leave them that way?* A sliver of panic found its way into my foggy brain.

"Sky? Is that you?" Mom rounded the corner from the hallway into the kitchen, and I sagged in relief.

"Yep." Normally, I would hang with Mom and talk, but I was so flustered from what had just happened with Damon that she would know something was off and ask me about it. And I was not sharing. "I'm super tired. Going to head to bed."

I dashed for the same T-shaped hallway she'd just left with the bathroom at the end and a bedroom on either side. "Fantastic job on Gia's hair. Thanks for saving her."

"No problem," she said with a yawn. "She looked good. I think I'll crash early myself. Have a good night, sweetie."

"You too!" I yelled before I shut my bedroom door.

Holy shit. I flopped onto my bed, bunching under my arms the watercolor-blue comforter that reminded me of the beach. I had no idea what I was doing. It was the first time I'd ever touched a penis. And it wasn't so bad. A smile curved my lips. He certainly liked what I was doing. And the kiss was spectacular, not that I would ever tell him. Part of me wished that kissing me was a daily request Damon had made to date Gia.

That was crazy. I needed to get Damon out of my head. I pulled my phone from my pocket, tossed it on the bed, and went into the bathroom. After brushing my teeth and washing my face, I changed into pajamas and crawled into bed. I wanted to read for a while and try to take my mind off him, if that was even possible.

I grabbed my book from the nightstand but didn't open it. Maybe I could think about all the things wrong with him. That might help to throw some ice-cold water on my raging inferno of need. Key word being *might*. It was all I had, and I mentally ticked off what was wrong with Damon.

1. He was a dumb jock.
2. I hated all athletes on principle, or maybe that was the same as number one?
3. He used girls and threw them away.
4. He didn't really care about Gia, and my best friend deserved better.
5. He was an alpha asshole.
6. Dominant, aggressive, and entitled.
7. So good at kissing—*wait!* That one didn't count.

My phone was blowing up, and since my list had gone sideways, I gave up and reached for it. I was sure Gia wanted to wax poetically about Damon some more.

It wasn't Gia. It was him.

I squashed the excited flame. I needed to stay mad. Because really, speak of the devil—or demon—and I ended up conjuring him. I needed to be more careful with my thoughts. But it didn't help that he was texting me, which inevitably put him back in my thoughts, no matter how hard I tried to banish him from there.

Damon: *Send me a naked selfie, and I'll ask Gia to eat lunch w/ me tomorrow*

Me: *NO*

Damon: *Fine—send a pic in your bra*

I laughed. That I could do. I rolled off my bed and changed into my most conservative black sports bra. It showed no cleavage, nothing sexy from me. Hello uniboob. I lay on the bed, positioned the phone above me, then snapped a pic and sent it off to him with a loud swoosh.

Damon: *Well played but your friend eats alone tomorrow*

I laughed then snapped a pic of my middle finger. He was such a prick.

Damon: *You want to fuck? I'm down for that*

Me: *Figures you would think that—fuck you*

Damon: *Put your hand down your panties. Bet you're wet from what we did earlier. Throbbing, soft, delicious*

I sucked in a breath and squeezed my legs together. He wasn't wrong. Not that I would ever tell him that.

Damon: *Send a pic of your hand down your panties*

They were soaked, and I moaned at the discomfort. The situation was getting out of control. I needed to stop. I switched my phone to silent then shut off the light. Somehow, I had to get some sleep, preferably without him appearing in my dreams.

When my alarm blared through my room like a thousand trumpets, I flipped my pillow over my head and groaned.

Fucking Damon. Most of the night, he'd texted, trying to bargain for favors, and I was the sucker who had kept peeking to see what he wanted next.

He needed to back off because I was exhausted and school was in—I lifted a corner of the pillow and glanced at the clock on my phone—an hour. I was screwed.

By the time I got to school with a giant to-go cup of coffee in hand, Gia was waiting for me and talking a mile a minute about how incredible Damon was.

"He's not that great." It slipped out before I could censor myself.

"Who's not that great?"

The deep voice sounded behind me by my ear. I didn't bother to turn. It was his fault I had barely slept. "That would be you. Just callin' it as I see it."

"Sky," Gia ground out.

I rolled my eyes as Damon's large hand palmed my ass and squeezed it. I turned my head to the side and sent him a death glare. He was damn lucky Gia couldn't see where his hand was, and he needed to move it fast.

I wrapped my arm around my stomach. "Ugh, I shouldn't have had that bean burrito for breakfast. Better back up, Demon, or I'll blast you."

Gia's face contorted in horror at my farting reference, but it had to be done. I needed him to get off me. The idiot only laughed. Too bad it didn't work, and I didn't have to fart. That would have been pretty sweet if I did. Bet he would give me some space then.

Damon crowded me more, seemingly leaning toward Gia. "Want to eat lunch with me, Gia?"

She looked at me, hesitation in her lack of response—why, I wasn't sure. I gave her a slight nod.

"Yeah, I really would." A brilliant smile lit her face. "See you at lunch, Damon."

Gah. I was irrationally annoyed. By her blindness and his hands. By it all. But mostly what I really wished was that Damon would stop touching me. I didn't want to like it, and I hated myself because I very much did like it.

When he took off, Gia started talking again about Damon, and I struggled to pay attention.

"I can't believe you said those things," she scolded.

"Why? You know I hate athletes. And he's not dating me, so who cares?"

"I just…" She wrung her hands. "What if he decides I'm not worth the trouble because you're such a ballbuster?"

I sighed. "Fine. I'll try to behave. But why did you look at me when he asked you to sit with him?"

She scrunched her brows. "Because we sit together."

"Oh." I grinned. Too much was slipping by me. "It's fine."

She bounced on the balls of her feet. "Can you believe he asked me to sit with him? I'll be at the table with the Elite." She squealed the last part.

I rubbed my temples and tried to feel excited for her. "Your plan is working out, despite the fact that it's Damon who's making it happen. Are you sure you don't want to date someone else?"

"Stop."

She smacked my shoulder, making my eyes pop back open. "What?"

"Sky," she huffed in exasperation. "He's a legend. So, no. I don't want anyone else. I know how you feel about athletes. But you can't lump him into the category where you stick all jocks, except for…" Her gaze darted along the hallway, searching.

A wishful gleam entered her eyes, and I couldn't help but wonder about it.

"Were you going to say Tucker?" *Does she still have a crush on him?* She had when we were in elementary school.

"Tucker is one of the few athletes you tolerate, or are even friends with." She shrugged then wrapped her hand around my arm, her long nails pressing down enough for me to pay attention. "Please give Damon a chance. There's so much more to him than you think."

Yeah, more than she knew actually. I grunted my half-hearted consent. "Fine. Whatever. I'll try to keep an open mind."

The bell rang, and we went our separate ways.

It wasn't until second period, in chemistry, that I had my next surprise. Damon sat in the chair my lab partner usually occupied.

I slid into my seat then hissed, "Get out. We're not partners, and what did you do to Erin?" I glanced back, but she was smiling happily at Brad, another one of the meathead football players who had been Damon's lab partner. Great, there was no way she would move back.

"This was easier, and everyone's happy with the new arrangement."

"Not me." I glared. "And that ass grab earlier will cost you a kiss for Gia." I stabbed him in the chest with my index finger, wishing it were a sharpened pencil instead. "On the cheek and in front of witnesses."

His very hot hand settled on my thigh, and I jumped. *What is he doing?* Then he moved it higher, and I sat there like an idiot, not saying or doing anything to stop him. *Why aren't I stopping him?*

His pinky dipped low and traced way too close. My hands clamped the table hard, and I shot him my most evil glare. I hated that I let him get to me.

He leaned close but didn't take his hand away. "What will this cost me?"

"More than you have to work with."

I shot a pointed glance at his crotch, and he removed his hand. It was a ridiculous claim, and we both knew it because he was packing in that department. It was my feigned lack of interest that struck home where it most counted—his ego.

The frown that formed on his too-handsome face told me enough. He didn't like that I still wanted nothing to do with him. I almost leaped off my seat and danced a little jig like Gia had done yesterday.

Chemistry dragged because I was entirely too aware of him. But he was moody, and that suited me just fine. Maybe I would even find Erin sitting next to me tomorrow.

When the bell rang, we went our separate ways without another word, which also suited me just fine. I almost slept through classes until lunch. After grabbing an apple from the line, I sat and watched Damon with Gia.

She sat next to him at the same table as Phoenix, Shane, and several cheerleaders—Tracey, Jessica, and a few others. We were rid of Piper and Brooke, as they had been seniors last year and were Cole and Riley's problem at Thane. It didn't look good, and I could already tell Jessica had it out for Gia.

Not once did Damon turn and talk to her or include her in the conversation. That asshole. He wasn't attentive or interested. All he did was talk to his cousins. After a few more minutes, Gia got up and came over to my table where we usually ate. She sat down and clasped her hands in her lap, her face pale. I was furious. He hadn't even looked up when she left the table.

"What are you doing?" I kept my voice low so as not to embarrass her any more. "You need to go back over there and make him pay attention to you."

It wouldn't work, though. He had been an asshat to prove a point to me about what would happen if I didn't act the way he wanted. I shook with anger.

"No." She sounded defeated, and I hated every second of it. "I'll just go to the library and get a book I need for class. I'll see you later."

"Okay." I didn't know what to say—*to her. Him?* I had plenty.

I stood and stomped over to his table as soon as she was out the door and on her way to the library. "We need to talk."

Damon's eyes slowly lifted to meet mine. His face was granite, and a muscle jumped along his jaw. "You know where to find me."

"Fine." I spat the word then marched out of the cafeteria and found the nearest stairs to the basement.

I stood in the middle of the dark and musty space, tapping my foot and fuming. The gross basement smelled like sweat and testosterone, two of my least favorite things. Dark energy charged the air, and I felt him. He barreled into the space with hostility blazing in every move. When he stopped in front of me, I almost stepped back—he was intimidating and so large— but I couldn't do it. No one would make me feel helpless, never again.

"The deal's off."

"No, it's not. You have to do this. You gave me your word." A ripple of panic went through me. It was for Gia, who had been there for me since we were little. I hated him even more for making me beg, but I would do it for her. "Please. Just name your price."

CHAPTER THIRTEEN

DAMON

#NamingMyPrice

Skylar was fucking hot when desperate. I didn't know what favor she owed her friend or why she would go to the lengths she was, but it meant I could up my ask by ten. I let my gaze wander over her slowly, taking in everything about her—the dark hair I wanted to wrap around my fist, her fucking insanely sexy lips, eyes that matched her name and stood out even more because of her hair color. And that ass, fuck, it was fine. She was slender and toned with curves in the right places. Not as curvy as her friend, which I was down with, too, though the girl talked too much, and I wasn't into her like that. *But Sky...?* She was a wet dream.

Still, her comment in chemistry told me how much she didn't want me. It burned. The only girl in school who wanted nothing to do with me, and I couldn't stop thinking about how much I wanted to do to her.

Across from me, and not close enough, she stood with her

arms crossed over her chest, anger emanating from her posture and expression. It only turned me on more. And having her in the basement, where I sparred with my cousins, lent a dangerous edge to what we were doing.

"I don't have forever," Sky snapped.

Her voice wobbled slightly. *Is she nervous?*

On the one hand, I wanted to see how far I could push her, and on the other, I didn't want it to end. "I want to get my fingers wet."

She sucked in air through her nose, and I laughed.

"I like it when you pretend to look appalled. It's convincing."

"Trust me. I'm not faking." She sounded unaffected, bored.

I knew better. Her responses told me otherwise. "Just so we're clear, you can say no. And when that happens, I hope your friend enjoys watching me take out Julie Parker, who willingly puts out."

"You're a pig."

I shrugged. "Never said I was otherwise. Do you think that prom queen crown is one-size-fits-all, or is it fitted?" *I love riling her.*

She huffed. "You're pathetic and disgusting. But since I don't have any other choice… fine."

Her hands went to her jeans, and she snapped the button free. I swear my tongue about rolled out of my mouth. But that wasn't the way I wanted it.

"Not here. Not like this." When I could put my hands and mouth on her wherever I wanted, it wouldn't be in the school's basement or even my car. It would be where I could lay her out, see and taste every sexy part of her, and make her see the fucking moon and stars.

She redid the snap loudly, then her hands fell to her sides in fists. "You have to apologize to Gia for how you acted at lunch."

"I planned on it." The only reason I'd ignored Gia was

because of Sky, not that I would let Sky know that. But damn, she affected me more than I cared to admit.

We parted ways. It was left unsaid when we would meet next, but I doubted I could wait past the night to call in what she owed.

The day dragged, and with each passing hour, Sky occupied more of my thoughts until she was all I could think of. Time to call her favor due.

I would wait to do everything I wanted to her later, in a better setting, but for the time being, she would fall apart in my arms from a simple touch. She didn't seem the type to hang around after school, which meant I needed to get to her fast. I stalked through the crowded hallways after the last bell rang with a single-minded purpose.

Increasing my stride, I rounded the corner that would take me to the school's main entrance and the hallway with Sky's locker. The crowd parted at the right moment, and I saw her long, dark hair as she slammed her locker and turned toward the exit. I couldn't let her leave, not when I had things to do to her. People moved out of my way as I closed in on her.

Curling my hand around her arm, I pulled her to the side then bent to her ear. "Meet me in the tower—now." Then I released her, noting how her blue eyes turned dark and stormy. Her lips pressed together, not detracting from how full and soft they looked.

"Here?"

Already turned away, I didn't bother with a response. The door to the stairwell yielded beneath my palms as I pushed it open, heading to the tower. It slammed behind me. I made it halfway up the second flight before a loud squeak sounded as Sky entered the stairwell. That door made an exuberant amount of noise, which served well as an alarm should anyone enter after us.

The third flight took me to the small alcove in front of the large front window. Anticipation climbed as she closed the distance between us until she stood before me, anger sharpening her features. It only enhanced her beauty and fed my dark desire to a nearly out-of-control inferno.

I hooked my finger around the strap of her backpack and slid it over her shoulder before lowering it to the ground. I had fifteen minutes until I had to get to practice, and I planned to use ten of them making Sky scream my name. But first, I needed to help her relax.

With my hands on her hips, I drew her close. Her eyes widened, and her lips parted with a gasp as she came in contact with my body. I was already hard and straining for her. I grazed the side of her arm before burying my hand in the back of her hair and slanting my mouth over hers. The small part between her lips was the perfect invitation, and I devoured her. Within half a second, she melted against me as I explored her.

Her breathy moan fed into my mouth, and I angled her head to deepen the kiss until she pressed against me, searching for more. With her palms flat on my chest, I kept her hands trapped until I was ready to turn her. My tongue tangled with hers, and I struggled to maintain some semblance of awareness of our surroundings. Just one touch and Sky could eclipse everything else, but I couldn't let things get too out of control due to the setting and time constraints.

So soft. I couldn't get enough of how she felt in my arms. How responsive she was—perfect in every way imaginable. I wanted to devour each inch of her, but I didn't have the luxury, not that afternoon.

I broke our kiss and pulled back enough to drown in her hooded, desire-filled eyes, inviting swollen lips, and how right her body felt against mine. But I had plans and gently turned her in my arms so her back was to my chest. We stood in front of a large window in the tower at the front of our school. People milled about as they talked or boarded the buses lined up along the curb, while others headed to the parking lot.

With the sun's angle, they wouldn't be able to determine who was framed in the windows—if they even looked up, which most people didn't. Sky wouldn't know that. The position would feel vulnerable, which would also work to my advantage.

I held her in place. My hand still fisted in her hair as I angled her head to the side and tilted it to take her lips in another drugging kiss. She relaxed back into me as I popped the button of her jeans then slid the zipper down. They were tight, and I had to release her hair to push them down her hips.

She broke the kiss and gasped. "What are you doing?"

I let her take in our surroundings, and her body stiffened slightly against mine.

"Cashing in on our deal. You asked me to keep paying atten-tion to Gia and not other girls, like Julie Parker, who are more than willing, so I want to get my fingers wet with you."

"You're crude."

I was, but she didn't complain.

"And you love it." I trailed my hand across her body then wrapped it around her delicate neck with enough pressure to hold her in place but not hurt her. She would be helpless as I played her body like a fine-tuned instrument, people moving like ants below us, all within her vision. I took away her control. All she could do was feel as I trailed my hand along her flat stomach then dipped beneath her panties.

I groaned at the first brush along her seam, enjoying the shudder that swept through her. Fuck. She was wet. She tried to cover her face, and I tightened my hold.

"Hands flat on the window."

"They'll see me."

I nipped at her ear, following the sting with a swipe of my tongue. "Maybe."

"I can't do this." Tension threaded through desire as her body tightened, stiff beneath my touch. She tried to close her legs.

"Open." I gripped her neck tighter, stilling her movement as she tried to free herself. "If you want to stop, I will, but then the deal's off. You're reneging on your end of the bargain." I pressed open-mouthed kisses to her jaw, wrapping myself firmly around her. My cock strained against my jeans, desperate to slide into her.

She eased her legs open and leaned fully against me as I crowded her toward the window. A shiver skated over her skin as I brushed my finger over her seam again, spreading the silky wetness as I went. Parting her, I groaned at how wet and soft she was beneath my touch. I dipped one finger inside her tight heat while my thumb traced slow, slick circles over her clit.

I built her desire in slow, agonizing strokes, sliding in and out, going deep and curling my finger, then pressing gently against her small bundle of nerves until she gasped and writhed from my touch. I moved my hand from her neck and nipped the slender curve, my moan vibrating along her skin as her sweet little body strained.

Fuck she was amazing. She made me feel alive, powerful, and completely fucking obsessed. Each touch, response, and sound she made imprinted on me to the point that I knew without a doubt that she was mine. All the games fell away, and all I saw was her.

I slipped two fingers in, stretching her slightly. Rubbing the silkiness of her come, I teased her clit with the heel of my hand until her hips moved in rhythm with me. I pumped deep inside her, curling my fingers until she shook in my arms.

Her breath increased in short pants, matching mine, and she rocked against me, meeting each thrust. Fingers spread against the glass, she remained open to me, and I took every advantage.

I cupped her breast through the fabric of her shirt, pinching her nipple then brushing my thumb over it. She whimpered, and I thrust my fingers faster. Her legs went weak, so I wrapped my arm around her and held her tight. When her hands left the window, she reached behind her until they threaded through my hair. She tugged on the strands as I increased the pressure against her clit.

"Damon," she gasped. Her breathy, hoarse voice exploded through the small space as her body tightened around me.

A wave of possessiveness rose in me as her orgasm coated my fingers, and I wished more than anything that I could strip us both bare and push my cock deep inside her willing body.

I cupped her sweet pussy, reluctant to release her. But as our breathing regulated, I withdrew my hand. She cried out, and my eyes closed briefly, savoring the feel of her in my arms before it was time to let her go. When I was sure she could stand, I helped her pull up her jeans and did up the zipper and button. Then I turned her around, and her teeth sank into her bottom lip as she observed me with wide, desire-filled eyes.

No words would be good enough between us. Not then. If I said anything, it would ruin what had just happened. I adjusted myself so it wasn't quite as painful, then took her hand and led her down the stairwell until we were at the first floor and the door that led to the hallway. We couldn't leave simultaneously, not when she wanted to keep us a secret.

She let me go, and with one last glance over her shoulder, she pushed the door open and stepped through. I waited a few more seconds then did the same, going in the opposite direction.

I still had practice, and I would be late with how much time I'd spent coaxing Sky to fall apart in my arms. It was worth every second, and I wanted to do it again immediately.

Practice ran short due to the coach's meetings, which worked for me. I planned to go home and eat, then maybe stop by Gia's and apologize. I could swing by Skylar's place after.

When I pulled into the driveway then the garage, I checked

to see if Dad was home. Raelyn's car was parked inside, but not his. I didn't have a huge problem with Riley's mom, but I had no desire to deal with my dad right then. I would be happy if he left me alone and let me graduate with minimal interaction.

I dumped my backpack in the mudroom and went into the kitchen. Louisa, our housekeeper, had modified hours since Raelyn had moved in last year. It was good, I guessed. Louisa was more like a mom to us, me more than Cole. I was glad she didn't have to work all the time. From what Raelyn had told me, Louisa's salary was the same, but she and my dad had thought that with a reduced workload—she only cooked anymore, and they'd hired a cleaning service—she could spend the rest of the time with her family. It was one of the only decent things my dad had done, so I didn't cause any problems.

I yanked open the fridge and rummaged around, pulling out some enchiladas. My mouth watered. I was starving from practice. A door slammed, and I looked up as Shane walked in.

"What's up?" I asked. "Phoenix with you?"

My cousins were over all the time. They ate with us along with their mom, who worked as an ER nurse. Aunt Cece was my mom's sister.

"He's at Monica's house since her parents are out of town."

"That a serious thing?" I doubted it.

Phoenix had the same perspective I did about dating. We didn't do it. Shane was the anomaly, and I guessed Cole too. But I liked Riley. She'd proven herself, so that wasn't too big a deal.

"Nah. Dish me some of that."

I pulled out another plate, piled it high, then microwaved both. We sat at the island, scarfing down the food. Louisa was a fantastic cook, and I told her so often.

"What's going on with the girl you brought to lunch? What was the point of that? Jessica's pissed, and you know that's not going to end well for the girl."

"Not really my problem." I shoved another forkful in my

mouth. "And her name's Gia. She's friends with that Skylar chick. Remember her? She was taking pictures and notes at our last practice of the summer."

"Oh yeah. She hates sports." Shane smacked my arm. "Tracey's afraid of her."

I grinned. "I have a feeling things are going to get pretty interesting at school. What does Tracey think she'll do?"

"Dunno," Shane said around a mouthful. "Something about Skylar doing something to some girl in elementary school. I wasn't listening. And who the hell cares anyway?"

"I'll have to find out from Sky."

The door slammed again, and I tensed. I hadn't checked my phone yet to see if Dad or Raelyn had texted, so I wasn't sure who was walking in. When Phoenix came into the kitchen, all my tension melted.

"Hey, what happened with Monica?" I ask. "You hit that?"

"Her parents came home unexpectedly. I bailed."

"You going back?" Shane pushed away his empty plate.

"Doubtful." Phoenix piled food on a plate, put plastic over it, then put it into the microwave. He leaned against the counter, crossing his arms, and his silver eyes zeroed in on me. "What's up with the girl at lunch today?"

Shane laughed. "I already asked him that. He still hasn't come clean. And remember the hot girl with black hair who came to our football practice and got under Damon's skin?"

"Yeah, Skylar McCormick," Phoenix said then grabbed his food from the microwave when it beeped. He joined us at the island. "What about her?"

My hand tightened around my water, almost as if out of jealousy. But that would be total bullshit because I didn't care about her, except for getting in her pants. Still, I wanted to know more, and Phoenix had a class with her last year. "What's she like?"

"She's cool, in a way. And she's smart. I heard from Noel Simon—"

"Doesn't Noel have a crush on you, Phoenix?" Shane laughed. "She hot, in a sexy librarian kind of way. What is she involved with? Debate team?"

"Aren't you dating someone?" Phoenix's gaze sharpened. "Or are you looking to branch out, finally?"

"Shut up. You know what I mean," Shane said.

I wanted to smack him for interrupting and taking the conversation in another direction. My cousins fell silent, and Phoenix went back to eating.

"No one cares about Noel," I snapped.

Phoenix didn't bother to look up from his plate and shoveled another mouthful in before responding. "And class president."

Fuck. I guessed we were still talking about that chick.

"So, did you sleep with her?" Shane pressed the issue.

"No. Noel's a guaranteed stage-five clinger," Phoenix said. "I'm not up for dealing with the persistence she'll show."

I'd had enough. "What did she tell you about Sky?"

Shane and Phoenix exchanged grins.

"Like a dog with a bone, man. She's really under your skin," Shane teased.

I was close to punching him. But he didn't have the answers I needed, and a fight would be another distraction. "Phoenix."

Phoenix swallowed another bite then set down his fork. "She got a scholarship to the academy. They only give one award per grade per year to students who can't afford the tuition. It's a big deal. Noel said she's gifted, or that's what she heard the counselors saying about her essay that won."

"I had no idea. But I can see her winning it." I was aware that she was smart, just not that she couldn't have gone to the academy without a free ride. But Sky lived with only her mom, so maybe they didn't have as much money to afford the academy as Gia's family. The academy wasn't cheap. We just didn't think about it because Dad paid my tuition, and our granddad covered the cost for my cousins'.

"I don't know." Phoenix downed half his water. "That's just what I heard. Lots of people like her, but Gia's her best friend. You already know that part, though."

"Yeah." And I would milk it for everything I could. "Sky's pretty protective of her."

"She's loyal." Phoenix's brows rose in challenge. "Are we any different?"

I snorted. "Whatever. I was just curious about the girl who thinks she can bash me on the academy's blog."

Shane grinned. "Tracey wondered why you haven't retaliated. It's not like us to leave something like that unanswered. Should I tell her it's because you want to get into Sky's pants?"

I grabbed an apple from the fruit bowl on the island and chucked it at his head. Shane's arm shot up, and he snatched it from the air before impact.

"Why does Tracey care so much?" I asked. "The only person she should be concerned with is you."

Shane rolled his eyes, not taking the bait. Phoenix went eerily still, and I knew he hoped my comment would get a rise out of his brother. I could push Shane, but I didn't want him storming out. Instead, I shifted my focus back to Phoenix. He had to know more. That Noel chick talked a mile a minute. I doubted that was all she'd said about Sky.

"Did Noel say anything else, like what Sky does outside of school or what she likes? Are they friends?"

"Friendly." Phoenix leaned back. "I don't think they're close friends. And I don't know. Probably books. Maybe movies? She takes as many writing classes as she can. People like that usually love to read too. Find common ground there. Or if you really want to date her, and not whatever this is with Gia and her, then take her to the movies."

"I'm not looking for common ground. Or to date her." I scowled.

"Then what do you want?" Phoenix asked when I turned back to them. "Because you're asking a lot of questions about some chick that you claim you're not interested in."

"She gets under my skin with how much she hates football."

"That's it? Or is it because she's not the type to fall at your feet when you snap your fingers?" Shane prodded.

His lips twitched, and I thought about launching more fruit at his head. One was bound to find its mark.

"It doesn't matter." Shane took a bite of the apple I'd chucked at him earlier.

"Why is that?" I asked, though I distractedly wondered what she read. *Romance books?* I could make that work. We could do some role-playing.

Phoenix smirked. "She hates sports, so she won't want anything to do with you."

"She may not like sports, but she likes me just fine." I couldn't leave it alone.

Besides, my cousins would take my secrets to the grave, so it wouldn't be that big a deal if I filled them in. Sky wouldn't find out, and her no-one-can-know pact wouldn't be affected.

"What's going on?" Phoenix narrowed his eyes.

I swore he was so much like Cole that it made my heart hurt. "We need to take a trip to Thane soon. Maybe go to a football game."

"We do. Now spill." That from Shane.

I filled them in on the sweet setup I had with Sky and how I didn't give a shit about her or Gia—but told both my cousins that they had better keep their mouths shut about it, and that included not saying a word to Tracey, Shane's girlfriend.

I couldn't see it ending badly for anyone. Well, maybe Gia. But so far, senior year was kicking ass.

CHAPTER FOURTEEN

SKYLAR

\#Fine

Finally, movie night with Mom. I settled on our worn couch, looking forward to spending time with her. We didn't get to do that often because of how much she worked. I studied her as she set up the movie. It was weird how much we looked alike, which I was grateful for.

She was too thin. I was already on the lean side, but Mom was on the I-eat-one-meal-a-day diet—and I suspected it was more from nerves of late. She had a ton of friends, who were more acquaintances, except for Gia's parents, who were close to her. Despite how gorgeous she was, she didn't date. Not for lack of invitations. She just never said yes.

And while we looked like sisters, I didn't feel as beautiful as she was. It was fine with me, though. I didn't care about that. I had plans, and they did not include a guy. Writing was my drug, and I planned to go places. It would already be an uphill battle if I went the reporter route in a male-dominated field. But women were constantly breaking the glass ceiling, and I would be one of them. So my looks, or lack of them, rather, didn't concern me —I was all about skills and craft.

"I like what you did with your hair," I said.

Mom had cut it so it fell just above her shoulders and framed her face with a few shorter, wispy pieces in the front.

"Thanks. This is easier for me to manage." She flashed me a smile then settled next to me. "Ready?"

"Yep."

She hit start, and I almost groaned. I hadn't been paying attention to what she'd picked. It was *Enough*, starring Jennifer Lopez. Great movie. I loved it, too, and could rewatch it many times. The problem was, I knew why Mom had chosen it. She was nervous and mentally preparing herself because Dad could be released from prison soon.

"You okay?" I cringed at my question, but she smiled and squeezed my arm.

"I am. I just had a craving to watch a girl-power movie."

"Okay." I let it go. Besides, I could get into it. I tossed my phone on the coffee table and kicked up my feet.

Movie night with Mom was something I loved. But my mind raced with unanswered questions. And the movie we were watching caused them to churn and multiply with lightning speed. Ten minutes later, I couldn't stop thinking about what next year would mean or where that would put Mom.

I pulled at a small string on the hem of my T-shirt. Mom and I liked to get comfortable in pajama shorts and tees for movie nights. Even though I was comfortable, something inside me couldn't relax, and the question burst from me. "Are you ever lonely?"

Mom grabbed the remote and hit pause. She shifted on the couch, bending one leg under the other, and she faced me, her back to the armrest. "Why would you ask that? I love our movie nights."

I studied the half-moons under her eyes that were only visible because she'd scrubbed the makeup off her face. "You never go on dates or talk about wanting to find someone. I just… I worry about you. You're passing up opportunities to let someone else into your life because you're worried about me or just too busy trying to make enough money to pay our bills. And if that's the case, you know I can help."

"Oh, Sky." Mom squeezed my arm. "I'm not lonely, and we're doing fine with money."

"Why don't you date anyone? I've never known you to go out with a guy. The only times you do anything outside of work, or spending time with me, is when you and Gabriella do something."

"I don't want you to worry about me. I promise I'm happy. But after everything with your father, I've realized I don't want to get married again."

"So?" I failed to see the problem. "You don't have to get married to find someone you like spending time with."

Mom looked over my shoulder, a faraway expression clouding her eyes. "Maybe someday." Then she swung her gaze back to mine with a clarity that told me she wouldn't change her mind. "But not now. I'm not ready. I don't have a desire to get involved with anyone. Maybe that'll change. Or maybe it won't, and I'm okay with that."

"I worry about you," I confessed one of my biggest fears. "I don't want to go away to school and leave you alone. Maybe it would be better if I went to the community college instead."

"You better not, Skylar McCormick."

"Full naming me, huh?" I teased, but there was no mistaking how serious she was. "Come on, Mom. It makes sense. We won't have as many bills because I'll be living at home, and we can do this"—I waved toward the TV—"as often as we want."

"We can do this anytime you come home to visit. But how do you know I won't start dating when you're out of the house? Hmm?" She raised her eyebrows, and that stubborn expression I was more than familiar with challenged me to contradict her. "I said I wouldn't marry again, not that I wouldn't ever date."

"I'm getting whiplash from this conversation." I was under the impression she wasn't ready. She'd just said she wasn't ready.

"I can change my mind."

I laughed. It was a joke between us. We were women. We reserved the right to change our minds without question.

"You're going away to school, Sky. It's important."

I dropped that part of the subject. "I don't think I want to get married either."

"Is that because of what happened between your father and me?" She frowned. "I hope that's not the reason."

"No. It's not. I'm not one of those girls who pictures herself as married with kids. I can't imagine it. I think Gia's dreamed of her wedding so much she's got the entire thing planned down to the placeholders."

"Light pink and white," we said at the same time then dissolved into giggles.

"I can't argue with her about the colors and what she imagines the venue will look like. And you would look stunning in the satin, off-the-shoulder bridesmaid dresses she's sketched and fixed into her dream wedding book." Mom smiled.

I scrunched my nose. "I can't think about wearing a light-pink dress, now or by her dream age of twenty-two, when she'll be at the altar with her Ken doll groom."

Mom's smile widened. "She's so much of what you're not."

"Right." I sighed, not wanting to think about that. Or what a mess I'd gotten myself into to make sure Gia had the senior year of her dreams.

"What I mean is, it's okay not to dream about a wedding. Or plan to have two point five kids and a house with a white picket fence. It'll either happen that way, or something different will. The point is to not close yourself off to the possibility of love."

"Spoken from a woman who says she's not ready."

Sarcasm bled from my words, and Mom lobbed one of the couch throw pillows at my head, which I barely caught in time.

"Fine," she said.

"Oh, fine?" I joked. "You're using that word? We both know what that means."

Mom rolled her eyes. "How about I make you a deal."

"I'm listening."

"I'll keep myself open to dating—"

"So, not an automatic no if a cute guy that interests you asks you out for dinner or coffee?"

"Right." She looked to the ceiling and blew out a breath. "I won't shoot this potential guy down if he happens to ask me out."

I grinned. "That's all I ask."

"Good. Now can we watch the movie?"

I nodded, feeling much lighter than when we'd first sat down to watch. If Mom said she would try, I believed her. If only the rest of my life would fall into place as quickly. She pressed play, and we both fell silent, easily getting into the story.

A half hour into the movie, my phone started blowing up. I swiped it from the table and barely stopped myself from growling. Damon was out with Gia and messaging me. Negotiating.

Damon: *Never stop using that cherry lip gloss*

Me: *R u drunk?*

I was done. I set my phone back on the coffee table, making sure it was turned facedown, and did my best to ignore it while it buzzed like a pesky insect.

"Everything all right?" Mom asked.

"Yep."

"What about school? Because I get the distinct feeling you're hiding from someone." She looked pointedly at my phone.

I rolled my eyes and gave her my best exasperated expression. "You're overreacting. I'm fine."

"Okay." She paused the movie. "Want some popcorn?"

"Yes, thanks."

She got up, and I grabbed my phone, intent on telling him to knock it off.

I swore under my breath. I had about twenty messages. Eighteen were from Damon, and two were from Gia. I ignored Damon's and read Gia's.

Gia: *Damon took me out tonight. He apologized for lunch. And tonight was going great, but then he got all moody and dumped me at home. No plans for another date. Please call.*

My finger hovered over the button to call her when another text came through. *You've got to be kidding me.* Damon was parked outside my house.

I needed to handle it quickly and shoved my feet into my shoes. "I'll be right back, Mom." Then I slipped outside and headed straight for his SUV.

Shadows darkened the side yard to an inky void between my house and Gia's without any of the windows casting light to lessen it. Clouds overhead obscured the stars, and even the sliver of moonlight did very little to dispel the night. Damon's car was off, his headlights extinguished, giving his presence a necessary clandestine aura, especially if Gia happened to look out her family room window. Good thing her room lay on the opposite side of the house, away from mine.

I went around to the driver's side, and he got out of the car before I could stop him.

"Ignoring me won't work, Sky."

My head snapped back. He was such a demanding baby. "Are you for real?" My hands found my hips and planted there.

"I'm doing you a favor."

His deep voice grabbed hold of me, but I resisted the pull and gave him another piece of my mind.

"If you're out on a date with Gia, you should not be texting me. That tells me you're ignoring her, again, and in direct violation of our deal." *Take that, asshat.*

"I paid attention to her just fine. But your friend is not my type, and I'm having to put up with her to get the bare minimum from you."

"She's beautiful. And guys like you give girls body complexes because you think only starving girls with big boobs are attractive."

He huffed. "That's not it at all. Physically, she's very attractive. It's her nonstop talking and attitude that aren't my thing. I prefer hostile and combative, wrapped in a gorgeous package."

I sucked in a breath. He confused me too much, and I couldn't determine whether I should be offended or turned on. *Maybe both?*

"But this isn't worth it. You're too much effort to pin down for the favor I'm doing you regarding your friend."

I shrugged, too heated to try to fix it. "Then quit."

Damon hauled me against him. He tangled a hand in my hair, and the other wrapped me tight so I felt every inch of his hard body. Then his mouth slanted over mine. I couldn't think, only feel. He took control, demanded, and I was helpless against the onslaught of sensations.

Kissing Damon was earth-shattering, and I was quickly growing addicted. When he broke the kiss and put distance between us, I was more than flustered.

"Why do you keep doing that?" It slipped out before I could stop myself. My brain wasn't engaged yet. He'd turned me upside down with one touch.

A slow grin transformed his face into pure gorgeous corruption. "Because I like it."

"Fine." I was rattled, and a thrill raced through me because I liked it too. "But you can't keep hurting Gia. You have to be the guy she thinks you are."

"That's ridiculous. The entire school knows I'm not the docile fantasy you're portraying."

"I don't care. Be attentive to her. And that means"—I ticked off the list of behaviors on my fingers—"no ignoring her. Treat her with respect. Be caring, and do all the senior year milestones I told you she wants."

A storm brewed on his face like I'd offended him. *What did he expect?* He was an asshole and should be the first to admit it. Why my telling him to be something different was such a big deal confounded me. But I was done trying to figure him out.

"You can be your usual asshole self with me, but be better with Gia."

"Fine, if you're willing and accessible when I call you."

What choice do I have? The jerk had me backed into a corner. "Within reason. I can't drop everything for you." I spun on my heel and rounded the truck, then walked backward to the house, needing to put distance between us. "This is one of those times. I'm watching a movie with my mom."

CHAPTER FIFTEEN

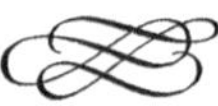

DAMON

#Secrets

It was late, but Sky was on my mind. In my room, because I was avoiding Dad and Raelyn, like usual, I sent Skylar a message asking if she'd gotten in trouble with her mom. It wasn't long until the three dots appeared with a single word—no.

I should have let it go, but I couldn't, and I pressed the button to call her. It wasn't what I would do with any other girl, but I wanted to hear her voice. And I wouldn't read into it.

"Hi."

I was almost surprised she answered. She was so prickly and combative most of the time. "Hey. How did it go with your mom after I left? Was she upset?"

"No." She yawned, followed by a rustling that could have been her getting into bed. "She wondered why I went outside and asked who owned the Range Rover, but that was it."

"Did you tell her about me?"

She snorted. "No. I told you before, no one can know about us."

Why does that annoy me? "It's nice that you spend time with your mom."

"Do you miss yours? That was a stupid question. Sorry. Of course you must."

"It's a fair question." I was so fucked in the head about it. "I didn't appreciate her when she was around. Things were… a struggle. I was team Dad, and Cole was team Mom."

"It's hard to look back sometimes, to wonder what you could have done. If anything."

"Yeah, trust me. It's on my mind a lot more than I would like. Mom struggled with depression. She was estranged from her family except her sister, my aunt. That wasn't her only issue. She wanted our dad's attention so much, but he didn't care about her as she did him."

"Are you sure about that? It's hard to have a clear view into someone else's relationship."

I sat on my bed with my back against the headboard. "Our dad was a cheater. Mom knew about it, but I didn't believe all the bullshit flying around. I assumed dad was just busy. He has businesses and clients all over the country, and her fears were so dramatic and, at the time, seemed delusional. My brother bent over backward to ensure she was okay, and Dad hired a nurse for when he wasn't around… but it wasn't enough."

"I'm sorry. It sounds like things were tough and you were in an impossible situation."

"I refused to see my dad clearly. It's on me." *And I'm afraid that I'm like him.* "I didn't call to talk about my family." I never did that, which probably wasn't healthy. "What did you and your mom watch?"

"*Enough.*"

"What's that?" I'd never heard of it. And I liked talking to

Sky, hearing her voice, so I planned to ask whatever I could think of to keep her on the line.

"It's an older movie, starring Jennifer Lopez, about a woman in an abusive relationship who takes back her life, and her daughter's, then kicks ass in the end. Mom likes to watch it occasionally, and because of my dad, it's been a regular in our go-to movie list."

"Your dad was abusive?" My hand clenched into a fist at my side.

"Yes. The lovely crescent scar on my temple is a souvenir from him."

Her voice had that clipped end-of-discussion quality, but I needed to know if she was in danger, because I fucking hated the thought of that. "Does he live with you?"

"No, he's in prison."

"Good." And because I sensed her discomfort with the turn of our conversation, I switched topics. "How did you and Gia become friends? You're very different."

"We've been friends since we were kids."

Her voice returned to the relaxed, sexy tone that I strained to hear in the hallways. That was what had brought me to call her rather than just text. I liked so many things about her. It was odd for me since I didn't normally associate feelings with my hookups.

"What happened with Gia tonight?" she asked.

"Nothing." That chick was just tiring.

"She said things were going great and then not so much."

"That was your fault. You wouldn't answer my texts."

"Huh. I'd never thought of you as needy."

"Guess you thought wrong 'cause I need a helluva lot from you." That was the kind of conversation I was more comfortable with, and just imagining Sky there to do anything I wanted or commanded her to do was the best turn-on.

"I'm in such high demand." She laughed.

"Do I need to worry about some big biker boyfriend coming for me?"

"No. No boyfriend."

"That's good." I sounded far more into her than I should. "I'm too pretty to be the one fighting instead of being fought over."

"You don't like fighting in the Ring? Why do you do it?"

I laughed as a surge of satisfaction buzzed through my blood at the thought of fighting then seeing Sky after, when the adrenaline would be at an all-time high. I couldn't wait for the next fight. I would have her wait for me in the locker room. "I'm kidding. I love to fight."

"I'll never understand boys. I've got to get some sleep. I have a job interview tomorrow at Chicks-N-Wings."

That place was a copycat of the chain restaurant with girls in tiny shorts and itty-bitty shirts. "No fucking way. You can't work there. It's demeaning."

"Says no guy ever—especially you, the alpha male king. Besides, it's about money. I'm not a trust fund baby. I have to work for what I want." A click sounded, and the connection went dead.

Fucking hell. I tossed my phone on my bed. Every forward step we'd taken had been erased. I was jealous, and she was defensive. But one thing would come from how we'd ended things. No way would I let her work there.

CHAPTER SIXTEEN

SKYLAR

#Jealousy

Chemistry was torture, and lunch wasn't much better. In chem, we had a quiz and weren't in the lab, so I didn't need to sit next to Damon. That didn't stop me from being aware of him the entire period. Or noticing how deliciously his blue shirt stretched across his broad shoulders or that I could practically see the outline of his abs.

When he walked past my desk, I got a front-row seat to the graceful way he moved for such a huge guy and how fantastic his ass looked in those jeans. And don't get me started on how his biceps flexed. If I painted or did any kind of art, I would want him to model for me, and I would enjoy every moment of it. He was a work of art—when he wasn't speaking.

I picked at my sandwich, unable to stop watching Gia and Damon interact at his table. She talked about something, one hand gesturing to emphasize her words, the other clinging to his python arm.

I'm not jealous.

But I was, and I hated it.

I tore off a piece of bread and chewed it slowly. I was just concerned for Gia. She could do so much better for herself, and I didn't want her to get attached to Damon. He would only hurt her.

During my study period after lunch, I got a pass to meet with the blog editor. I hurried through the halls to the media room we used when it was free, like then. Mitch, Josie, and Anne were already there. I dumped my bag on the floor and must have fallen into one of the seats slightly too dramatically because they all turned to me with curious eyes.

I shrugged then directed my attention to Stephanie, who sat facing us on one of the desks. *Please tell me I'm off sports.* Since Dan had graduated two years ago, Stephanie had been lobbing the sports coverage to each of us. I'd covered most of the girls' sports last year, which had been fine. That was also where I'd met Riley, who was dating Cole, Damon's brother. Both were in their first year at Thane University.

I liked Riley a lot. Too bad Cole's brother was such a tool and the bane of my existence lately. Stephanie started the meeting by assigning the new teacher article to Josie, who did a lot of personal-interest pieces. Mitch got the music write-up. Our band would be going to some big concert competition and master classes for the weekend—sort of like state championships but for music, I guessed. I would've researched the hell out of it had it been assigned to me. But since it hadn't been, I didn't waste my time thinking about it.

"That leaves baseball for you, Sky."

"What?" I shouted and slammed the flat of my hand on the top of the desk. "No. Give it to someone else, or I'll walk."

Stephanie pursed her peach-colored lips—*and on that note, ew, peach?* That was a choice.

"Fine," she said. "I forgot about your little hang-up."

Not so little. I imagined jabbing my pen into her eye. Mean, but that was how much I despised all things baseball. And I wasn't Stephanie's biggest fan either.

A devious gleam entered her eyes, and her thin lips quirked up as if she were holding back a grin. "You'll take football then."

Fuck me. It'd been a setup. I grinned back at her because I had an ace up my sleeve. "I'm not sure I can. I have a job interview today." I shrugged and did my best pouty face. "I'm sure Anne would love to do it."

Stephanie glared. Anne was a sucky writer and did a shit job of researching, which left her without the right questions to ask or the ability to craft the best article.

"No. It stays with you. Tell your job that you can't work during home games."

Stephanie directed her dictator glare at Mitch. "You'll cover the away games, and Anne will take the rare practice we need to run a spot on."

I could barely pay attention to the rest of the meeting.

Gym was ridiculous. I didn't count it as a class, nor should the school. I had a high GPA, but it could affect my score if I didn't get an A in gym, which pissed me off. Not everyone was an athlete.

I sat in the bleachers with Gia as her teacher went over volleyball rules we all knew. Both our gym classes had been combined for a tournament of sorts. Having her in class with me, even temporarily, was the only good thing about it.

Banners with years of wins for sports ranging from football to golf hung from the ceilings and on available wall space above the bleachers. Every once in a while, I glanced in Jessica's direction. She sat next to two sophomores, Tina and another girl whose name I couldn't remember. I didn't like the evil look on Jessica's face or the sheer glee on the other girls' faces either. They were plotting something, and I needed to keep my guard up.

Gia elbowed me, and I turned toward her. She hated athletic stuff just as much as I did. Neither one of us was exceptionally skilled at team sports. As names were called, people trudged down the steps to get into their designated teams. That was better than having a captain who picked their teammates—one thing to be happy about anyway.

"I hope we're on the same team," Gia whispered.

I snorted because that probably wasn't the best idea. "We both suck, though."

A smile flitted around the edges of her lips. "Who cares? We would have more fun that way."

She wasn't kidding.

"Gia Moretti," her gym teacher called in his deep tone. Visually, he searched until his eyes landed on Gia, who'd jumped at the sound of her name.

My hands curled around the edge of the bleacher seat. After another few minutes, I was called. I grinned because luck would have it that we were on the same team. It sucked for the athletic kids on our team, but it would make class go by faster for us.

From the corner of my eye, I kept track of Jessica and her younger minions as I made my way down. Her expression held a calculating twist to her lips that I wouldn't ignore when we played against whatever team she was on.

Another few minutes, and the rest of the teams were established, and we were assigned courts in the fieldhouse. Rachel Jeffers appointed herself captain of our team. No one opposed since she was on the actual volleyball team.

We got into formation and would rotate positions whenever she told us to—*or after someone made a point?* I wasn't listening during the rules or when Rachel said what we were doing. She had to point to a spot on the floor when I stood in the wrong place. *Ugh.* I wasn't usually so helpless. It was just one of those days when I would've loved to blow off school and stay home reading all day.

A whistle blew, and the games were underway. I did my best to stay out of range of the ball, as did Gia. I caught her eye a few times and shared a sly smile. We might actually be okay. Rachel was kicking ass, as were the three guys on our team. It took the pressure off Gia and me.

"Skylar!"

Shit. I instinctively held my hands up. The ball hit my open palms.

Jack dove in front of me when the ball bounced off me and went nowhere. His fist made contact, and the ball was airborne. Rachel leaped up and spiked it to the other side. Our opponents missed, and it was a point for us. Rachel and Jack turned and glared.

I shrugged. They'd learned I sucked. *Yay, team!*

I would have to fake a sprained ankle or something and be forced to write a paper on volleyball for a grade rather than participate. I was okay with that. *Why can't we pick and choose what we want to do?*

I shifted to where Rachel barked for me to go, my mind still wandering. I was fine with swimming, yoga, or anything involving running. Team sports were the problem. Hand-eye coordination, maybe. Or I just wasn't a team player. That was probably the majority of the problem.

We shifted positions again after Jack scored, and I found myself at the net. Gia was in the unfortunate position of serving the ball. I winced when her first attempt flopped and fell shy of the net—on our side. She tried again, and by some miracle, the ball made it over by half an inch.

Our teammates compensated for us by getting into our space and taking the shots, hits, spikes—whatever the correct term was—instead of me or Gia. Things were going well until we rotated opponents. Jessica got into position on the other side of the net from Gia, who was in the back, middle for the new match. *Or is it game? Who the hell cares?*

Jessica's team had the ball. The serve sailed over the net, and Mark's fists set it for Rachel. She jumped and spiked it over the net. *Impressive.*

Gia and I did our usual—staying out of play as much as possible. Until Jessica jumped up, her palm smacking the ball hard. She put power behind the spike, and the ball shot past the front line. The ball slammed into Gia's head with a loud thud. My mouth dropped open. A couple of our teammates cursed or inhaled loudly. Gia stumbled back a step, her eyes slightly out of focus.

I whirled around. Murderous thoughts filled my head as I stomped to the net inches from Jessica's pert little nose. My mouth opened to rip her to shreds when a shrill whistle stole my moment. Gia's gym teacher appeared out of nowhere and ushered her off the court. He asked her a series of questions, looked into her eyes, then told her to have a seat and keep track of the score.

Fuck this bullshit. When the game resumed, I did everything possible to hit the ball, aiming for Jessica. I was highly ineffective. But it was therapeutic for my rage. It went from explosive to a slow, roaring boil. The rest of the class went by in a blur.

When the whistle blew again, signaling class was over, I helped Gia up, and we went into the locker room together.

"Are you okay?" I asked.

"Yeah." She grimaced. "More embarrassed than anything. A slight headache, but that's it."

"You know that was intentional, right?"

Gia grinned. "Probably. But it also means she knows I'm with Damon now and is pissed about it."

"And that's a good thing?" We changed out of our gym clothes then stuffed the uniforms into our lockers. The sound of metal clanging filled the large room as well as laughter and muted conversation.

Gia shrugged. "I don't know. But it tells me that she recognizes Damon is into me, that we're dating, and she's mad about it."

"Are you going to tell him? Maybe he'll do something to stop her from being such a bitch." Or he would if I talked to him. I might do that if I didn't get a chance to set Jessica straight myself. I glanced around the locker room for a glimpse of her.

"No, I don't think so. I'm okay. I see no reason to get him involved."

She pressed her lips together then grabbed her book for her next class, hugging it to her chest. I slung my bag over my shoulder, stopping short when I caught sight of Jess.

"That was a bitch move." My voice rang clear, stopping her and her two minions in their tracks.

Jess slowly turned, and I sensed rather than saw Gia shift slightly back and behind me.

Twisted laughter spilled from Jessica's red lips. "Like it? You both can expect a repeat of that for the rest of the tournament."

"You don't scare me." My words were quiet but filled with menace.

"I should. I'm just one of many who will make your life miserable—if I want to." She winked. "I'm still debating over it. See, the thing is that I know Damon very well. We've been hooking up for a few years now."

"You and how many other girls?" I tilted my head.

Red infused her cheeks, and hatred flashed in her eyes. "He's not exclusive. I'm aware of that, but I'm the only constant. And your girl Gia? She's a joke. I can't even take her seriously. No one else will either."

"Watch your back, Jess. We've already had this discussion. I can make your life just as miserable as you're threatening to with us. But a dethroned mean girl is just a target. Might want to rethink what you're gonna do." I notched my head toward her cohorts. "Your up-and-coming social climbers there should think hard over their next step and reconsider. They're fair game by association."

My grin was slow and wide. I'd delivered my kill shot, and it had hit home by the widening of her eyes and how she whirled on her heels and left. I had plenty I could work with to humiliate her through the blog if I needed to.

I turned to Gia, a buzz singing through my blood from the confrontation, then I paused. "What?"

She was shaking, her olive-toned skin a sickly, pale shade. She sucked in a breath and patted her chest, her eyelids lowering for a few seconds before she calmed enough to answer. "I don't know how you go up against people like her. I can't. She's terrifying."

I'd never understood that about Gia. "She's just a person. She doesn't have any more power than you. Stop putting her on another level."

Gia shook her head. "I don't know, Sky. We're different that way, you know?"

Sadly, I did. I was the one who had defended her when Sarah had pushed her on the playground, and I'd gotten detention for punching her in the face.

"What will you do to her?" Gia's voice was quiet.

"Nothing right now. But if she pushes either one of us, I'll publish something unflattering about her. I'll highlight her bullying and how she tripped Melanie at the game when they were going onto the field."

"You have a picture of that?" Her brows raised.

I laughed because, yeah, I did. Moments like those—I made sure to document them. I didn't normally use them because I didn't see the point. No one wanted their worst moments displayed for everyone to see. But that ball was in Jessica's court. If she pushed me and did something to Gia, I would retaliate. I was sick of her viperous attitude.

"Maybe don't do it? Things could get so much worse if you do," Gia said.

"You want me to go along with whatever Jess does? Just roll over? What if it's only to you? Are you just going to smile and deal with it, not say one word, never push back?"

She shrugged, and I wanted to throw up. I would defend her until my last breath. Not much had changed with Gia's lack of a backbone. I wondered if it ever would. I wouldn't always be there to be her voice, though. Someday, she would have to fight her own battles.

Classes went by with agonizing slowness. After school, I met up with Gia at her locker to complain about the article for that weekend's home game. I didn't bother to bring up what had happened in gym again. When she wanted to, Gia was fantastic at sticking her head in the sand.

"I don't see the problem. We can go together. It'll be great." Gia smiled wide.

"Not great. I have zero interest in football."

"But Damon will be there. He's an amazing player. And I'll be there too."

I hiked my bag higher on my shoulder. "Fine. We'll go together."

"Great. And maybe we can grab something to eat with Damon and some of the other players after." She grabbed my wrist, laughing when I hissed and backed away. "Stop it. It'll be a fabulous opportunity to get interviews out of the way."

That wasn't a bad idea.

"What interviews?" Damon stopped next to Gia. His gaze locked on me.

"Nothing." I shot Gia a glare. No need to give him more information. "I've got to run so I make it to the interview on time. Talk to you later, Gia." *And fuck you, Damon.*

I didn't miss how thunderous his expression grew.

I couldn't help but chuckle as I walked away. His look was

priceless, and he couldn't do anything about his fury because we had a deal. And if he went back on it and was a jackass to Gia by interrogating me and ignoring her or showing how little he cared about her, he would lose out.

But so will she.

It was a sobering thought. Her stupid list was ridiculously important to her. I couldn't let my piss-poor attitude sabotage it. With a sigh, I got in my car and headed to the restaurant interview—which went amazingly well, and I was hired on the spot. I loved Lizette, the manager. And the uniform wasn't as bad as Damon had said. The shorts were tiny, but they were the same as the Nike Pro athletic shorts the cheerleaders wore. The T-shirt was tight and ended just above my waistline to show a thin strip of skin, but it wasn't low cut, and it had cap sleeves. Plus, they were both black with the restaurant's name in white on the shirt.

I shadowed another waitress for the dinner shift, helping where I could. It was busy, but no one grabbed me or was rude. If a table looked like it might get out of hand, Lizette shadowed us until they got the hint, and she was a big woman, not one to mess with.

I was exhausted by the end of the shift, and when I walked to my car, I groaned at seeing Damon parked against my door.

"Are you a stalker now?"

He smirked. "You're pretty full of yourself. I'm only here to pick up dinner for my family." His gaze crawled all over me.

I was still in uniform, and suddenly, what had seemed decently modest left me feeling like I wasn't wearing anything.

"The interview went well?" He said it with a frown.

I was well aware he wasn't pleased. "It's none of your business."

He pushed off my car door and stepped closer to me. I used his movement to angle toward my escape.

"You could work many places where you don't have to show off your tits and ass."

"Fuck off." I opened my door, threw myself inside, and slammed it shut before hitting the locks. I didn't spare him a glance as I started the car and sped out of the parking lot. The nerve of him. I wasn't showing off anything that most of the girls in our school didn't reveal in gym class.

Mom wasn't home when I got there. Still angry, I dropped my stuff in my room then took a shower. When I got out, a text sounded from my phone.

Of course, it was from Damon.

Damon: *I just don't want people calling you the names that they call the other girls who work there*

Me: *Thanks for your fake concern*

Damon: *I can pay you if that's what you want to be*

Uuugh! I threw my phone—at the bed because I wouldn't break it for an asshole like that. Then I stomped to it, shut it off, and tried to breathe through the anger. I could get through the next few days without committing murder.

Tomorrow is another day.

CHAPTER SEVENTEEN

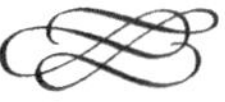

DAMON

#Done

Gia had no idea she was a fake girlfriend. The chick was clingy. I clenched my jaw, my only outward sign of annoyance, as she hung all over me, blabbering about something I didn't pay attention to.

We had an at-home football game the next day and a fight Saturday night. And on top of all that, I had a crazy amount of homework due Friday. I shouldn't be out, but I couldn't concentrate knowing Sky was at Chicks-N-Wings, working, so I'd dragged Cole, Riley, Phoenix, and Shane along. My brother and Riley were home for reasons I hadn't bothered to find out. I was just glad to see them. And as a bonus, Tracey hadn't joined us. She and Riley didn't get along, probably because Tracey was scared of Riley, which was another thing I liked about my brother's girlfriend—who was also my stepsister, since her mom had married my dad.

None of that mattered. What did was watching Skylar

interact with her customers. I was beyond irritated by it. And if any of the guys at the table she served got handsy, I would slam my fist into their faces.

Sky looked incredible in the tight, tiny shorts and shirt. All black fit her personality. Her dark hair was in a high ponytail, not something I'd pictured for her because she usually wore it down. It accentuated the graceful curve of her neck. What I didn't like about everything I had just admired were the guys around her doing the same thing.

A week had passed since I'd talked to her. She had switched her schedule around, so we weren't in chemistry together as another attempt to avoid me. During that time, I hadn't taken Gia out either, which meant I'd had no excuse to get my hands on Skylar or even message and call her.

We were seated in her section, but she'd passed us to a different waitress. After placing our orders, I shrugged Gia off—who clung to me like a cheap suit. Her cloying perfume gave me a headache, and how she grabbed my arm was awkward and unwanted. I bet she'd never given a guy a hand job in her life—probably never kissed a guy either. The mention of a blow job would probably make her crazy blond hair explode.

I couldn't take being ignored anymore. "Skylar."

My voice boomed across the restaurant, making her turn in our direction. I left her no choice but to come to our table.

"Hi, guys." She pasted on a fake smile, stood by Gia, and pretended I didn't exist. "Need anything?"

"I need to know how you like being objectified."

Finally, she looked at me, cold fire and hatred pouring from her tightly clenched lips. "No one's objectifying me."

I snorted. "Bullshit, your table of five over there is staring at your ass. Or do you like that? If that's the case, bring it on over here."

She placed her hands on the table and leaned toward me, a storm darkening her blue eyes. "Fuck you, Demon."

Her use of my nickname was a nice touch. "No thanks. Looks like you've got plenty lined up and willing since they're already checkin' out the goods."

Her hands balled into fists, and she physically jerked away. I laughed, but it sounded hollow even to my ears. The girl had fight in her. If she weren't at work, I had no doubt she would have tossed one of the many drinks at our table in my face.

Gia, for once, was quiet. That didn't sit right with me. All the shit Skylar was willing to do so her friend could have the senior year she'd dreamed of, and not once had Gia defended her. It only drove home how much the chick wasn't my type. Our table was quiet. Phoenix, Cole, and Riley glared at me. Shane watched Gia.

"You need to chill," Cole said.

I could tell Riley and Phoenix wanted to lay into me, and it pissed me off. I nudged Gia. "I'm outta here."

When she stood, I guided her out of the restaurant and into the car.

She remained silent on the drive home, which only made me angrier. "I won't be able to meet you tomorrow night after the game. I need to get some sleep."

Big brown eyes collided with mine when I pulled up to the curb in front of her house. She looked like she was about to cry. Why, I had no idea. Because if it was about me not wanting to hang out as opposed to what I'd said to her best friend, she needed to get her head on straight.

"What about Saturday?"

"I might have some family shit to do." It wasn't true, but I wouldn't share that with her.

Cole might've caved about Raelyn and Dad, but I hadn't, and I wanted nothing to do with them.

She hesitated, unsure. I knew what she wanted—me to kiss her, which she hinted at by leaning forward. When I didn't, she sat there for another few seconds, probably waiting for me to walk around and open her door. I wasn't doing either of those things. Instead, I turned up the music, a rude hint for her to get out of my SUV. When she finally did, I pulled away, not even checking to see if she made it to the front door.

I had a game to concentrate on.

CHAPTER EIGHTEEN

SKYLAR

#Squad

With the tray balanced on one hand, I delivered food to the table Damon had pointed out as the objectifying one. I kept my distance with a bright smile on my face. In and out, that was the goal with them. I spent more time, and genuine warmth, on most of my other tables, especially the elderly couple.

Damon had left with Gia in tow. I was furious with her, too, and planned to have words when we were alone. *How could she have sat there while he was a complete douchebag to me?*

"Sky," Riley called to me as I passed their table blessedly lacking Damon and Gia.

I paused then moved closer. "Hey, Riley." My cheeks heated with embarrassment that they'd witnessed the bullshit going on between Damon and me. "Can I get you guys anything?"

"Can you sit for a minute?" She leaned into Cole, who had his arm draped over her shoulders.

"Sure." I took the spot where my best friend had sat since I had a few minutes between checking on my other tables. Nervous as fuck, I grabbed the end of my ponytail before realizing I was fidgeting. Releasing my hair, I clasped my hands in my lap.

"What's going on with you and Damon?" A frown marred Riley's gorgeous face.

Cole and Phoenix looked at me with interest while Shane shoveled the rest of his food into his mouth.

I shifted uncomfortably, trying to figure out what I could say that would appease them. "He's dating my best friend—"

"The girl who said nothing when Damon was being an ass?" Riley snorted. "Girl, you need new friends. I hope you know none of us approve of how he treated you. Right?" She narrowed her eyes and met each of the guys individually.

Cole and Phoenix smirked, but it didn't bother me. I knew Cole would support whatever Riley felt strongly about. Last year, they had gone from enemies to inseparable, and I'd witnessed him warning guys off her, obsessed and deeply in love.

Phoenix, another prime example of a player like Damon, showed signs of depth I hadn't wanted to see. Mainly because he was one of the Elite. But from the little I'd forced myself to pay attention to during the Riley-Cole debacle last year, I found that he was very observant. I'd caught the dissention between the two guys over how Cole had treated Riley. Of the two brothers, I worried Phoenix would see through what was going on behind the scenes between me and Damon. If that even mattered. It probably didn't, because I couldn't see him ratting me out to Gia.

Shane was a bit of a mystery, but I suspected he wore blinders. He was too invested in Tracey, and she was a bitch. That was a strike against him in my book, not to mention they were all athletes.

Riley was the exception. I genuinely liked her. Especially since the day I had interviewed her after her first spectacular diving meet. She'd asked me not to print any pictures of her face. It had spoken to something deep inside me, specifically the padlocked Pandora's box filled with what I didn't want to remember or couldn't that I kept buried.

"Gia isn't the most confrontational person. I'm sure she said something to him when they were alone." I wasn't. That was a bald-faced lie. And by the looks on all their faces, they didn't believe it either.

"He's not into her. So, what's really going on, Sky?" Phoenix put his elbows on the table and leaned forward.

"That chick isn't my brother's type." Cole's steady gaze was too intense.

"It's the article I wrote about him. He's been pissed about it and giving me little jabs like today since it went up on the academy's blog."

That was true. And they would know it too. Damon definitely would have bitched about it to them. They were his family and best friends. A pang hit my heart because I knew how tight they were. They might disagree with how Damon treated me, but they would have his back in everything that mattered.

"That makes more sense, but the way he looks at you doesn't mesh with that," Riley grinned mischievously. "Something hot is going on between you two."

She held up her hand to stop me when I opened my mouth to deny it.

"You don't have to admit to anything." She and Cole shared a knowing look. "Just know that I'm thrilled you'll be part of our group. And, Sky?"

"Yeah?" I stood because one of my tables had raised a hand to get my attention.

"We don't let anyone fuck with one of us."

Fierce brown eyes met mine, and I felt rather than saw that the guys backed her words. A shiver danced over my exposed skin from their group's powerful and determined energy. A part of me longed for what she said to be true, that I belonged with them. But I didn't think Damon would agree.

CHAPTER NINETEEN

DAMON

#Bros

When I got home from dropping Gia off, I heard Raelyn and Riley chatting in the family room. Dad was on the phone in his office, and I suspected he'd decided to get work done so they could have time alone. Which was what I wanted with my brother. I found him in the basement with a game on the TV.

"Hey." I fell onto the seat diagonally from him, the game still in view. "How long are you in town?"

"We have a few days off school. Riley and I wanted to catch your game."

"You have a bye week?"

"Yeah, and she didn't have meets either." Cole muted the TV. "What's the deal with you and the blond chick? She's not your type."

"I like blondes."

"Sure. But not clingy, obsessive ones. And that girl screams stage-five clinger from a mile away."

"Phoenix and Shane didn't fill you in?"

Cole grimaced. "Yeah, I know about your deal with Sky to date Gia, fulfilling the girl's senior year list. What I don't get is why you would do it. You and Sky... you hated her last year."

"Sky is... tempting. She drives me crazy, and when she came to me about helping her friend, I couldn't pass up the opportunity to get into her pants." It sounded crass as hell. Usually, I wouldn't care, but a small part of me rebelled at talking about her like that.

Cole said nothing, but his look unsettled me. He saw too damn much, and I didn't like it.

"How's football and Thane?"

He grinned and relaxed back on the couch. "It's hard as hell but amazing at the same time. Riles and I are so busy. Both our sports are like a full-time job. Then fit in classes and studying around that. It's a lot. I love it, though. You need to hurry up and get there. I miss the hell outta you."

"What are the guys like?"

"Better. Their mentality is either the same or similar to mine. We're close, more like a family than a high school team."

I was ready for it. "I'm tired of it here. Time can't move fast enough."

"You say that, but when you get to Thane, you'll want it to slow down."

"Maybe." I kicked my feet up onto the coffee table.

"What's new with our cousins, anything?"

I snorted. "Nothing. Phoenix is focused on football, and no girl can get her hooks into him for more than a night, which drives Tracey oddly crazy. She seems to want to hook him up with a friend. Shane's still whipped. And did you know that Tracey is afraid of Riley? That was a fun tidbit I learned."

Cole's laughter filled the basement. "I'm not surprised.

Nothing Tracey and her friends did could get under Riley's skin. All their efforts to intimidate only amused her."

"I've always liked her. I'm glad you pulled your head out of your ass."

"Bullshit, you didn't like her initially, either, or when I told you who her mom was."

I tossed a pillow at his head. "You're projecting. I defended her a few times. She had our backs when you tried to blame her for throwing that party in our house and left the mess for Dad to come home to. If you would've looked at the crap you did to her and her reactions, like how she hadn't ratted us out, you might have pulled your head out of your ass sooner."

"Whatever. We had a rough start. Things are better than good now."

"What'll happen when you go into the NFL?"

My brother was destined for that path. It was what he'd always wanted, and he had talent in spades.

"We'll figure it out." His green eyes shone with determination. "She's the one. Besides, she's an Olympic hopeful. Wherever we end up, we'll find a way to accommodate a coach and the type of pool and boards that she'll need."

Cole *would* too. If he set his mind to something, it would happen. Riley was a lot like him in that respect.

"How's Coach?"

I shrugged. "Fine. I was late one day for practice. I don't know if he'll start me in the game this weekend." It'd been worth it. The feel of Sky falling apart in my arms had starred as a running fantasy in my mind far too often.

"You're kidding, right? Phoenix will only have Shane as an option without you. Johnston is a mediocre second-string running back."

"I know. I'm trying not to stress about it. But I'm glad you're home for a few days anyway. Are you coming to the fight?"

"Probably not. It's too much of a risk for Riley and me if we get caught. You should think about that too." He stared at me for too long with his eerie intensity that felt like he could see all my secrets—the darkness that lurked just below the surface and fed on violence and sex. "How are things at home?"

"They are what they are." I didn't want to get into it.

"Dad hasn't said anything, but your less-than-receptive attitude hasn't thawed toward him and Raelyn. Why?"

"You know why." Instantly furious, I used my words as weapons. "I can't believe you're on their side. He cheated on Mom with her. She was so unhappy she took her life. How can you forgive him for that?"

"Because it's Riley's mom. I had to take a step back when the shit hit the fan and reevaluate. He's human. His marriage to Mom wasn't for love. It was because she got pregnant."

"So you're saying his cheating was right?"

"No." Cole ran his hands through his dark hair. "I'm saying they had too many things stacked against them. Mom loved him so much more than he did her—if he ever had. Then there's Raelyn and how Dad is with her. I try to see things from an outsider's point of view. When I look at everything that way, I can understand. You should try it. Dad isn't the enemy."

Wrong. Dad was. And I was just like him, destined to cheat. The only thing worse would be if I had ended up like Mom, destined to love someone more than they loved me.

CHAPTER TWENTY

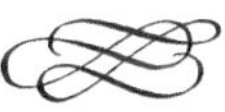

SKYLAR

#Ick

What the hell, Gia? I tugged my hair with one hand and white-knuckled my phone against my ear with the other. Embarrassment threaded through the hurt from how she hadn't defended me while Damon was being such an ass.

The phone continued to ring. It wasn't that late. Damon would have taken her home from the restaurant long ago. I knew she wasn't out with him, judging by his pissy attitude. Standing in the glow of the parking lot's streetlamp, I hung up and hit the button to call her again. She finally picked up on the fourth ring.

"Hello?"

Fuck that. She knows it's me. "Why did you just sit there? Damon was a total dick, and you didn't say a word."

"You weren't being that great either. You dumped our table onto another waitress."

"No shit. Because of the sort of situation that took place.

What's going on with you? We're friends." As a couple exited the restaurant, I stepped out of the light and toward my car. I felt sick to my stomach about the tension between us.

"It doesn't help that you're arguing with my boyfriend. What if he decides it's not worth dating me because you're being a bitch to him every time we turn around?"

I stopped several feet from my car, shock rippling through me like she'd reached through the phone and bitch slapped me. "Then he isn't worth it." When she said nothing, I growled through my shock and pain. "What you're saying is that he's more important than all the years of our friendship."

"That isn't what I said," she snapped, irritation clear in her tone. "But you could drop the attitude. And... you know I'm not good with confrontation. You usually stand up for both of us. I wasn't aware things had changed overnight."

Something certainly has. "This is a clusterfuck, Gia. Is he really worth it?" I could feel our friendship slipping away, and I hated every second.

"Yes." Her voice cracked across the line. "I told you how much this means to me, and if you care about me at all, you'll drop the bitchy attitude toward Damon and support me in this."

The line went dead. I pulled it away from my face and checked the screen. Sure as shit, she'd hung up on me. Fuck my life. *My patience is thin enough as it is, and she wants me to dig deeper?* If only she knew the lengths to which I'd gone for her. Maybe she would appreciate me more. I snorted. *Now, who's the delusional one?*

I briefly shut my eyes and released the tension and anger from the call with Gia. Things weren't as bad as I'd made them out to be. *So what that Gia's spineless sometimes?* She was my friend. She had plenty of qualities that more than made up for what had happened at Chicks-N-Wings. Besides—I felt the thick stack of dollars in my pocket—things were looking up in some ways.

A hundred dollars richer, I crossed the rest of the parking lot with a wad of cash tucked securely inside my purse. I hadn't bothered to change into different clothes, so the end of the night had been easy. I'd finished my closing responsibilities, given the bar a percentage of my tips, and headed out. If only I could erase the uncomfortable conversation with Gia, I would consider it a successful night. Sort of. Damon's gripe about me being objectified wasn't far from my thoughts.

The job was okay, but I hated to admit that Damon was right —and I wouldn't tell him. Comments *were* made that I had to bite my tongue about, like when an old man had told me he wanted to be served by the prettiest waitress. I'd struggled to hold back a resounding "fuck you." And some douche seated with what looked like fellow frat jerkoffs had almost grabbed my ass.

My mind still reeled from the conversation with Riley. She was good people, and I liked her a lot. But I wasn't meant to be a part of her group. The guys had been careful about what they'd said to me. Not Riley. I suspected she would lay into Damon when she saw him next.

Damon and I were using each other—not much more to it. Still, I loved how he was with his family. It was his one redeeming quality I could admit. And how he made me feel when he touched me, but I would take that secret to my grave.

I only hoped he would stay far away from my job while I worked at the restaurant. The money was good, but I wasn't sure I could hang in there. Mom wasn't happy. She didn't want me to work, just focus on school. But her birthday was coming up, and I wanted to get something nice for her as well as take her to that steak restaurant she'd mentioned. It was way out of our price range.

I felt the weight of my purse, and satisfaction made the night almost worth it. My aspirations weren't too far out of our reach anymore. A couple more nights like that, I could deliver everything I wanted to give Mom for her birthday.

After unlocking my car, I flung my purse on the passenger side and got in. The car was old, without a Start button like Damon's SUV. His came with every possible upgraded option. I turned the key—and nothing happened. Taking a deep breath, I tried two more times. *Fucking Damon.* My car's lack of response had him written all over it.

I yanked my phone from my purse, hands shaking with rage, and had to retype the message twice from how hard I was hitting the keys.

Me: *What the fuck did you do to my car?*

Three dots appeared, and I called him every name I could think of as I waited for his response. *Fuck it.* I couldn't deal with him. I shut off my phone, too upset to read whatever excuse he had, and got out. I locked up, fixed my bag so it hung across my body, and set out to walk home. It would take me a good hour on foot. At midnight, I wasn't happy about that, but no way would I wake Mom up to get me. And ordering an Uber wasn't an option. I needed every penny for Mom's birthday surprise.

It was dark and not necessarily the safest idea I'd ever had. Yanking the band from my hair, I released it from the ponytail and ran my fingers over my scalp, easing some of the tension from having it up. I preferred it down, which meant wearing it up hurt like hell toward the end of my shift.

A few cars passed, but when one slowed beside me, I tensed to run.

"Get in," Damon snapped in that deep, commanding voice.

I refused to look at him or the fancy SUV he drove. "You treated me like shit. I would rather get murdered in the street than get into your truck."

"Get in, or I'll call Gia. Right now."

I snorted. *And say what?* "Go ahead."

He kept pace beside my fast walk and called Gia, putting the phone on speaker. When she answered, her voice sleepy, I tensed. He muted the phone and looked at me with raised eyebrows. The ball was in my court.

What would he say? I swung my gaze to him, horrified. He could ruin everything just out of spite—that goddammed asshole. I yanked open the door and got inside with a huff. A satisfied grin curved his mouth. He hit the button to unmute his phone.

"Hey, Gia. I just called to tell you that I'm sorry for how I acted earlier, and I wanted to say have sweet dreams."

"Oh, that's okay. And thanks, they will be now." Her voice was husky.

I didn't like it, and I glared at Damon as he sped up and headed toward my house.

"I know you said you're busy on Friday, but do you want to go out to breakfast Saturday morning?"

"Is that a date?" Damon asked, his voice playful.

"If you want it to be, yeah. I hope so."

The fucker knew he had me with that one, and his cocky gaze said everything he didn't. He left Gia hanging, waiting for a response from me. But I planned to get something out of it, too, so I nodded.

"I'll pick you up Saturday morning then. Good night."

Gia's breathy response was full of hope, which hit me with a crushing sense of guilt. But I was involved in the whole thing, so when he popped the snap on his jeans—clearly, he expected something from me right then—I scooted closer.

I undid the zipper to slide my hand inside and around his long, thick hardness. He pulled into the park by my house again —the place would never be the same to me.

Then his hand tangled in my hair, and he gave my head a slight push. I released him and shoved him back. "What the hell do you think you're doing?"

His thumb stroked my lower lip, and I hated how tingles followed in its wake. "I want to feel your mouth on me."

"No. And if you try to shove my head again, I'll punch you in the balls. If I want to suck your dick, I will. Are we clear?" I wouldn't move until I got a response.

"I have something to look forward to, then."

"In your dreams, maybe." I smirked, but my stomach was a mass of nerves. Something about Damon was so beautiful, despite his shitty attitude. And even with the guilt over our agreement, a thrill raced through me. It was bad because I was essentially lying to my best friend by touching him or allowing him to kiss me. It was to get her what she wanted so desperately that she was willing to humiliate herself—like I was one to talk—but she would see it as a betrayal if she ever found out. I had to make sure she never did.

He pulled me closer when I took him in my hand for a second time. I shivered at the contact. His hand was in my hair, and he angled my head again. That time, I paid closer attention to what I was doing. The silky-smooth feel of him contrasted with his hardness. Then he lifted me, and I instinctually straddled him. It gave me the freedom to use both of my hands while he framed my face.

I cupped his balls when he slid his tongue along the seam of my lips. When he thrust into my hand, I opened my lips for him, letting him explore my mouth. It was erotic and out of control. Both my hands grasped him, and I pumped up and down.

He devoured my mouth, making me wonder what he would be like if he ever went down on me. Then he groaned and pushed harder into my grip. Hot come spurted all over his chest and my hands.

When he broke the kiss, my mouth felt swollen and violated in the best possible way. He grabbed a shirt from the back and handed it to me. When I was done, he took it from me and cleaned himself up. The entire time, I couldn't take my eyes off him. The angles of his face held such raw beauty, the heat of his dilated eyes as he watched me, his body's powerful build.

But he's not for me. I eased off him and climbed over to the passenger seat. His gaze followed me, and I sucked in a breath at the banked desire reflected within.

"Do you want me to get you off?"

His deep voice rasped over my body in a sensual caress.

"No." I locked down how tempting that sounded, how my body softened at the thought of his hands or mouth on me. I couldn't keep doing this. Hardening myself and my voice, I said what I had to. "Fix what you broke, then deliver my car to my house by the end of the weekend." I wrestled with my keychain, almost breaking my nail getting the house key off it. I grabbed his wrist, turned his hand over, and slapped the car keys against his palm.

His fingers curled around them, and I released him, my skin tingling uncomfortably from that brief touch. He said nothing. I didn't care. I needed to use my final dagger, and he'd better take it to heart.

"And then I never want to see you again."

CHAPTER TWENTY-ONE

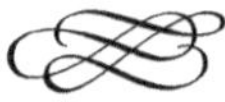

DAMON

#AllAbouttheThrill

Phoenix, Shane, and I were early to the field. It was always like that. Game day kept us going no matter the shit going on in our lives. In sweats, I stood in the end zone, visualizing how the game would go—the arc of the ball as it soared through the sky, my fingers plucking it out of the air to tuck it securely to my chest, then kicking in a burst of speed to the end zone.

I settled into a quad stretch. Shane and Phoenix did the same —stretching and their own visualizations. We all wore earphones and went through the routine of our separate pregame preparations.

The evening was gorgeous. The sun was still out. And when it set, the stadium lights would go on. It would be a long weekend for us since we had a fight tomorrow night, but I needed both to burn off some steam.

Time moved slowly then sped up as we filed off the field to get taped and dressed. We did more stretching with the team, followed by drills. Close to game time, Coach pulled us aside for a pep talk and last-minute instructions.

For the home game, the stands were crammed with people from our school and their parents. The opposition's fans peppered the bleachers opposite the home side. Special teams took the field after we won the coin toss to receive. I could barely stay still on the sidelines as the ball was kicked and flew through the air. Meyers caught it at the twenty-yard line and ran it for a gain of thirty.

Adrenaline flooded me as I took the field, lining up with the rest of the offense, anticipating the snap of the ball and Phoenix sending it soaring. Phoenix lived for football. It was deep in his blood, like it was for my brother. Shane and I loved it, but football wasn't everything to us, like it was for them. Exhilaration pumped through me, and I changed with the ball snap, becoming a machine as I ran a variation of my route. I ended up where Phoenix needed me, the ball falling into my hands at the right time and place. Then I turned up the speed and sprinted full throttle to the end zone.

The crowd was on its feet—the roar deafening. I tossed the ball to the waiting ref and got ready to do it again. We went for the two-point conversion. The ball snapped, and Phoenix faked to Brad, the tight end. Shane was open, and Phoenix fired a bullet at him.

The stadium exploded in cheers as we got off the field. Shane and I didn't waste time on celebrations or dances when it was what we were supposed to do. Score, let the defense do their thing, then get on the field and do it again. It wasn't the same for a few of the other players. All it took was a word from Phoenix, and that shit stopped. In place of showboating, their determination and focus snapped back into place.

I scanned the crowd after ensuring our defense held the field. I found my brother easily—then Sky. Holy fuck. She sat next to Riley in the stands. Color stained her cheeks, and she smiled wide. *Stunning.* When she found me on the sidelines, our gazes locked, and everything else disappeared.

She was so close and yet not close enough. I wanted to go to her. If it weren't for Shane knocking into my shoulder and shouting to get on the field, I would have pushed through the crowd to approach her.

As I lined up, I couldn't help but wonder if she'd come specifically to watch me. With a herculean effort, I breathed in the smell of grass, systematically recentering on what I needed to do until I saw only the opposition, my teammates, and the end zone.

I maintained enough concentration to respond to the snap, plowing through a block and running the route Phoenix needed me to. Sky was still there, blanketing my every thought. She was who I wanted to celebrate with when we secured the victory.

CHAPTER TWENTY-TWO

SKYLAR

#GameDay

The academy's blog has been the bane of my existence lately. *Cover the home games, Sky.* As I climbed the outdoor stadium bleachers at our football field, Stephanie's nonnegotiable voice rang in my ears from our brief editorial meeting that morning. I'd gotten out of as many of them as possible, but she'd put her foot down. So, there I was, looking for a seat in the full-to-capacity home section.

Did the entire school show up? I shuddered at the thought. It wasn't my scene. As my gaze scanned the rows looking for a spot, someone waved. Riley. I grinned, more than happy to sit with her and Cole. I didn't have as much of an issue with him, only because of how much I liked Riley.

I climbed the short distance, as they were only a few rows up, and wove through the small space while people moved their knees to the side or stood to get out of my way. I fell into the seat she'd saved me.

"I wasn't sure you would show." Riley grinned. "What made you change your mind?"

I didn't need to tell her that I was basically allergic to athletes. She'd gotten that from our first encounter last year. "I have to cover the game for the school's blog."

I rolled my eyes, and she laughed.

"It should be a good one." She looped her arm through mine and leaned close. It was loud around us already since the team had taken the field. "Are you going to tell me what's happening between you and Damon? I know something's up. The attraction between you two is crazy. I have no idea how that other girl didn't notice it."

Because Gia chooses to be oblivious? I wasn't sure, but it worried me. "Nothing is happening between us."

Riley snorted. "Keep telling yourself that."

I tried to, but it got more complicated every time he touched me. "How's college life? I'm guessing it's vastly different than the shitshow that's high school." I was over the year already. Gia's senior list had done me in from the start.

"I love it." Riley's smile was contagious. "I never thought I would be able to go, and I miss my mom like crazy, which is why Cole and I come home whenever we can. Will you go to Thane?"

"Yeah, I think so."

"For journalism?"

I shrugged. "Yes, but maybe something else too. I haven't decided. I want to write, but expanding into other areas like computer science would be a good idea for marketability."

"I'm sure you'll figure it out."

I braced myself against the mischievous sparkle that flared within her brown eyes.

"Damon is into you. I know I keep going back to it, but I'm telling you, he can't get you off his mind."

"Probably because we can't stand each other."

She snickered. "Yeah, sort of like how Cole and I were."

I pushed out a resigned breath. She wasn't wrong there. But I didn't want to talk about Damon. "How's Cassie? Is she still dating Matt?" I got along well with the laid-back guy in their grade—he had a total surfer vibe.

"Yeah, those two are attached at the hip. I would be surprised if they made it to senior year without getting engaged. They're going to Hawaii for spring break to surf. We weren't invited, which should tell you everything about their trip."

"I'm not surprised. I thought they could go the distance right from the start of them dating."

Phoenix threw the ball, distracting us. I wanted to hate the game, but the adrenaline danced through my veins as the ball soared down the field only to be snatched out of the air by the tips of Damon's fingers. I held my breath as I scooted to the edge of my seat. He tucked it into his body and put on a burst of speed, outrunning the opposition's outstretched hands into the end zone. I jumped to my feet and cheered with the rest of the fans.

Holy hell. That was intense. They lined up again rather than kick a field goal, and I tensed, chanting in my head to the football gods for a favorable outcome. It was so unlike me, but I was helpless against the sheer talent on the field. Phoenix, Damon, and Shane were leagues above the other players. They didn't showboat or seem to hold themselves apart while on the field. The entire team ran like a well-oiled unit. A testament to Phoenix, as the QB was a leader, which he was to our team.

The center snapped the ball to Phoenix, who dropped back, found Shane, and tossed it for an easy two-point conversion. I'd researched the game enough to know the ins and outs of the positions and rules. I needed to do the blog articles justice so no one on the team would come calling for my head after I fucked it up. Footballers had egos. Damon was a perfect example.

Each call the announcer made went down in the notebook I

had perched on my leg, pen at the ready. As players did some-thing notable, or if they didn't, I recorded it, jotting down names.

I'd never thought I would find myself in the bleachers, watching a football game, let alone cheering on our team. They were incredible. Even I had to admit that.

My fingers white-knuckled my pen as we intercepted the ball. Riley and I jumped to our feet, yelling with the rest of the fans as Shane, who occasionally played defense—*who knew that happened?*—sprinted down the field, the ball tucked against his chest.

I shoved my hair from my face and grinned. Endorphins flooded my body, and fuck it. I was enjoying the hell out of the game.

Damon came off the field with the rest of the offensive line, and I could barely tear my eyes off his powerful form, though Riley nudged me.

"I'm texting you the dorm I'll be in next year so you can request it. Or Cassie, you, and I could get a three-room suite."

"You're not living with Cole?" It seemed odd that she wouldn't.

"Not until third year. The rest of the guys have to live in the football house, and Cole needs to be with them. We're getting a place for all of us after that."

"Okay, and thanks." I didn't commit to dorming with her, though I wanted to. Things felt too up in the air. *And who knows?* I might have to be very careful about staying far away from Damon next year if things imploded. It seemed like they inevitably would.

Home, the glow from my laptop's screen taunted me, and I scrubbed my hands over my face before setting in front of it. I had an article to write, and I was torn for the first time since covering guys' sports of any kind. I still hated athletes, but I couldn't deny how intense the game had been or the unmistakable talent on the field.

I had to stay true to my journalistic integrity no matter how resistant I was to feeding the guys' overinflated egos. I glanced up to the side of Gia's house just beyond my open window. There wasn't much to see since it was dark, but I wondered what she was up to. Things had deteriorated between us, and I had no clue how to fix it. I wouldn't write the post to try appeasing her. It was time I reported the cold, hard facts.

And for some reason, that settled my churning stomach. I rested my fingers over the well-worn keys missing some of the letters from overuse or my nails scraping the paint off and got to work.

Hidden Valley Academy Eagle Eye Blog

A Blowout Win
by Sky McCormick

HVA Eagles' 67 to 19 blowout win against archnemesis HVP Tigers showcased the sheer talent of the home team. Despite taking the field with the loss of Cole Savage, Thane University starting tight end, the combination of our remaining star players, Phoenix Bennett (QB), Damon Savage (RB), and Shane Bennett (RB), solidified what an unstoppable force they are on the field.

A myriad of events came together, including a blocked punt by special teams player McKenna, an interception by Shane Bennett, and consistent short runs by Jackson (TE) that added to the points scored. Was it just the starters who pulled off this stellar victory against our rivals? No. Quarterback Phoenix Bennet threw for a record nine touchdowns, utilizing the second-string players in the final quarter with a seven-yard gain by Montgomery (TE) that resulted in a touch-down. Our defensive linemen Tillman and Vickers demonstrated quickness and power as they stopped runs and rushed the Tigers' QB. The facts remain that our Eagles' varsity team played hard and played to win.

What does this mean for future games? If the Eagles continue on this path, another title is likely within their grasp.

CHAPTER TWENTY-THREE

DAMON

#Landslide

Skylar had come to the game, and it was all I could think about after. We had crushed our opponents on the field by a landslide. Her presence had pushed me to be faster, better, and unstoppable to the point that she couldn't ignore me and post a slandering piece, like last time.

Phoenix's arm had been on fire, and he'd thrown six touchdown passes to me, Shane, and Brad, our tight end. The crowd had been intense with every hard-won QB tackle, touchdown, and field goal.

I was hoping for a one-on-one interview, but Sky had left before I came out of the locker room.

I was wired—and so glad I didn't have to deal with Gia and her nonstop chatter. I'd talked Shane and Phoenix into going to the gym, the hole-in-the-wall one, not ours at my house. The less I was home, the better.

"Did you see Julie Fisher?" Phoenix added weight to a bar

then situated himself on the bench. "Jeff broke up with her, and she's on the prowl."

"You gonna hit that?" Shane dropped the weights he'd been squatting. "She'll probably be at that party on Saturday before our fight, and Tracey wants to go there first."

"I thought maybe tonight, after we work out. Julie's a fun chick. I could probably text her on my way home."

"Fun how? I only vaguely know who she is." I finished my reps and sat on the bench, still restless.

Phoenix put the weights back on the racks. "She's up for anything when she's not dating someone and doesn't take herself too seriously."

"You may want to watch out for Jessica." Shane removed his weight belt from his waist. "Tracey said she's furious you're dating that Gia chick."

"You know what's up with that." I didn't want to say anything specific since we were in a public gym.

"Yeah, but she doesn't," Phoenix answered. "And Tracey's a bitch. I bet she's egging Jess on."

"What's your problem?" Shane growled. "Stop saying shit about my girlfriend."

"Whatever, I'm heading out." Phoenix texted as he went toward the exit. "Later."

"See you for our run tomorrow." I needed to work on my endurance, and he was brutal about making Shane and me do Saturday runs.

"Why did you say that?" Shane frowned. "I don't want to run. We have a fight. It's enough."

"I don't want to, either, but we have to be prepared for this summer. You know preseason workouts at Thane will be hell. Cole already told us everything we needed to expect and where to prepare that he thought we were lacking." Shane would hate my next statement. "And it's not Phoenix but the two of us who are slacking on running."

Shane ignored me. I didn't care. He would fall in line in the spring. I would too. We all knew I was full of shit about wanting to run anyway.

"I'm gonna take off." I couldn't stop thinking about Sky. I had to see her. I didn't care if it was one in the morning.

"Yeah, me too. I'll see you tomorrow."

We walked out to our identical black Range Rovers, and he took off in the direction of our subdivision while I headed toward Sky's. It bothered me that the last time I'd dropped her off, she'd jumped out of my truck before it had even come to a complete stop.

I parked farther from Gia's place, toward the end of Sky's property line. It didn't matter that much. The houses and lots were small. Sky's appeared to be even less square footage than Gia's. I shut off the engine and shot Sky a message to come outside.

If she ignored me, I would go. It wasn't like I could knock on the door at that time of night. The ping from my phone surprised me.

Sky: *Go away*

I couldn't stop from grinning. She wouldn't have texted if she didn't want me there. *Fine.* I could play her game. I responded by *asking* her to come outside that time. I even included a please.

My gut tightened as I waited for her answer. When a few seconds passed and nothing came through, my anger brewed. Then the door opened, and she rushed toward the SUV. She wore sleep shorts and a baggy T-shirt, but that didn't detract from how sexy she looked. Sky had legs for days. I wanted to wrap them around my waist and bury my hands in her long, silky hair. She was even more beautiful with no makeup on, not that she wore much anyway. Her smooth skin glowed, and those lips—I was obsessed with them. I got hard every time she was near.

She opened the door and climbed inside. I didn't know why I was there. It wasn't like we were good for each other. She hated me and what I represented, and I didn't have the best outlook on women. But neither of us was looking for a relationship. It was a mutually beneficial exchange.

"What do you want? I'm tired." Her eyes drooped sleepily, and she looked so damn soft and sexy.

I shrugged. "I just got done at the gym and didn't want to go home yet. I thought we could…" I couldn't believe what I was about to say. "Talk."

"Are you feeling okay?"

She pressed the back of her hand to my forehead, and I grabbed it, brushing a kiss along the inside of her wrist before releasing it. Her pupils flared, and her luscious lips parted before she snatched her hand back. The scowl returned, the same one I was becoming intimately familiar with and had come to expect from her.

"I'm fine," I said to answer her question. "Where did you go after the game?"

She yawned. "Home. I wrote the article for the blog and sent it off, as I was supposed to. I hate sports, by the way."

"Yeah, I'm aware. Did you slam me again?" It only mildly bothered me. The more I got to know her, the more it seemed like her disdain toward athletes held a deeper meaning.

"No." She sighed. "You were on fire tonight. All of you guys were."

I laughed softly. "Are you coming over to the dark side?"

"Hell no. I hate it, but Stephanie's forcing me to suffer through the home games."

"Who's she?" Maybe I should send her flowers for making Sky watch me play.

"The editor for the blog, who was appointed by my creative writing teacher, not her peers. We're short a sports writer since Dan graduated two years ago. I did women's swimming and diving last year, and this time, she cornered me into covering football."

"How did she do that? Couldn't you have stayed with what you did last year?" I remembered she'd covered Riley's meets, and the pictures Sky had taken had always obscured her face. They were images of Riley diving but only when her face was turned away.

Riley liked Sky a lot. She'd let me have it when I'd eyed Sky for a moment too long last year. My brother's girlfriend was tough, and I'd backed off because I owed her for keeping her mouth shut about a lot of the shit Cole had done to her. But things were different now.

"It is what it is. Besides, the diversity of what I have to cover looks good on my college applications."

"Do you want to major in journalism or English in college?" I couldn't imagine doing what she did. Nor did I want to.

"Probably journalism. But I don't know. Creative writing is pretty great too." She yawned again.

I moved the console back, motioning for her to come closer, then chuckled at her glare. "I won't do anything. You can rest your head on my shoulder, and I'm warmer." The goose bumps on her legs hadn't escaped my notice.

She thought about it for a second then scooted closer, and I situated her with her back to my side. Wrapping an arm around her, I rested my hand on her flat stomach.

"What about you? You're going to Thane too? That's where Cole and Riley are, right?"

"That's the plan, and I wish it would come sooner. Being away from my brother is hard. We're close."

"What about Riley? Are you friends with her now?"

I smiled. "Yeah. She's my stepsister."

"Oh, that's right. I forgot your dad married her mom this summer. Do you get along with her mom?"

"Raelyn's all right, but I'm not cool with some history

involving her. So, no, to answer your question. I try to stay out of her and my father's way as much as possible." It was weird to tell her such personal stuff, but I liked talking to her.

We talked for another hour, and I kept things light, never going too deep into her family life because I knew something very dark had happened with her parents. And I feared if I'd touched on it, she would bolt. Having her in my arms was incredible, and I didn't want the experience to end.

When she fell asleep, I continued to hold her, content to remain in the SUV together for a little while longer. Eventually, I followed her and finally nodded off.

The sharp rap against the window jolted me awake, and my arm tightened around Sky. Then the door opened, and my vision focused on the woman with dark hair and blue eyes who looked so much like Sky that I had no doubt she was Sky's mother.

Shit, this isn't good.

"Sky." Her mom's voice cracked through the silence, and Sky stirred.

"Mom?"

I helped her sit up, then she was out of my SUV without even turning to say bye. Her mom fixed me with a sharp look as Sky shut the door then tugged her mom inside the house. I got the hell out of there.

Once I was home, I went to my room, stripped, and fell onto the bed with a vague sense that I had forgotten about something, but I was too tired to care what it was.

It was afternoon when I woke up to several messages on my phone. Rolling over, I read through them. Phoenix ripped me a new one for blowing off the morning run. Shane had sent me angry emojis. I guessed he'd gone.

Then there were some from Gia wondering where I was. *Right...* I was supposed to take her to breakfast. I shot off a reply.

Me: *Sorry—got the days mixed up and slept in*

Gia: *That's okay*

I rolled my eyes. If that was Sky, she would have come over and blared an airhorn or something equally unpleasant to wake me up rather than roll over and take the shitty way I'd treated her.

Me: *Come to the fight tonight bring your friend*
Gia: *I'll be there!!!*

I sent her the address. I was playing a dangerous game but couldn't resist the thrill.

CHAPTER TWENTY-FOUR

SKYLAR

#Possession

"He's amazing and so sweet." Gia continued to sing Damon's praises. "He even called me and apologized for skipping breakfast. I guess he was so tired from the game Friday night that he overslept."

I grunted. The real reason was that he'd been parked in front of my house for most of the night. Everything was getting more complicated, and I felt out of control. It was dark out, almost ten at night, and I was bone-tired. "Why do I have to go? The fights are stupid. Just a bunch of rich kids beating the crap out of each other."

"You're going because you're my best friend, and..." She whipped open her closet door and jammed her finger on the ridiculous senior year list. "Get invited to the Ring."

I rolled my eyes then flopped onto her bed. "Yay, you did it. You got invited. Nowhere on there does it say we have to *go* to the Ring."

"Your sarcasm is duly noted and rejected." She grinned over her shoulder then went back to applying her mascara. "We're going."

I couldn't help the sigh that escaped my mouth. The web I'd spun twisted around me in an intricately dangerous design, where I felt like the prey rather than the engineer.

"I'm pretty sure I'm his girlfriend now." Gia fluffed her blond hair. She hadn't straightened it, and her natural curls gave her a different look than how Mom had styled it.

"How so?" I frowned. Though I was happy for her, my stomach tightened uncomfortably at the thought. "Did he ask you to be his girlfriend?"

"Well, no." She pursed her lips. "But I've been sitting with him at his table during lunch, and he hasn't allowed that horrible Jessica girl to cling to him. That says something right there."

My focus sharpened, and everything in me hardened. "Has Jessica or Tracey said anything mean to you?"

Gia only shrugged, refusing to meet my eyes in the mirror. Red stained her cheeks, which was confirmation enough. It looked like I would have to stick to Gia like glue on Monday and smack Jessica down several pegs. I looked forward to it, which was much better than worrying that my plan to help her was imploding.

"Are we driving to the fight together?" I didn't bother asking where it was because I already knew from friends who liked to go. And I'd gone with Trent once before.

Unlike most of his friends, Trent was a student council member who liked living on the edge. I enjoyed having friends from different cliques, and it helped to get information for articles.

"Gia. How are we getting there?"

She stared dreamily off into space and snapped back to reality at my sharp tone. Alarm bells blared in my head.

"Oh, I thought we could Uber to it."

"Fine." I knew why she wanted to go that route. She hoped to get a lift from Damon after. Not me. I would catch an Uber home, too, unless I could get someone I knew to take me, which was preferable to spending money on a ride.

She messed with her phone then looked at me for probably the first time that night.

"We have five minutes until our ride's here. Is that what you're wearing?"

I grinned. "I don't have anyone to impress. Besides, nothing's wrong with my outfit."

She snorted. Whatever. I was comfortable in my ripped jeans and faded black T-shirt with distressed white stars scattered over it.

Getting out of the house proved a challenge, but Gia overcame it by telling her parents a friend had invited a few girls over to her house, including us. Such a little liar, but it took one to know one. My gut churned again with that last thought.

When we got to the obscure warehouse in a sketchy area of town, we stuck close then joined another group waiting by the entrance. Two big wrestlers manned the doors, and they waved us through without a problem when it was our turn. I repressed a shiver, thinking I would never get over the dark and dangerous feel of underground fights.

We pushed through the crowd for a better position, and when we glimpsed the ring, we staked our claim on that spot. I didn't get it. For all the rich boys taking their aggressions out on one another, they sure as hell hadn't picked a posh place for it.

I nudged Gia then nodded toward a group of girls passing around a flask. "I didn't realize this was bring your own beverage."

Gia grinned, but her attention was immediately diverted. She grabbed my arm in a death grip.

"Ow." I peeled her fingers off me. That would bruise.

"There he is. Oh my God. Look at him without a shirt. He's perfection, and I want to lose my v-card tonight." She thumped my shoulder with her open palm.

"Is this how tonight's going to go?" I smacked her hand away. "The fight's over there. It's not about beating my poor arm until I'm black and blue."

She had the decency to look sheepish, but it didn't last. "I see Phoenix and Shane."

"And Tracey." I couldn't let her forget about the bitch squad.

Jessica had to be close by, along with whatever new minions had filled the open spots in their group from Piper and Brooke graduating.

"I don't care. I'm going to go stand by them to support Damon better."

Christ. I rolled my eyes so hard that I almost gave myself a headache.

"Come with me," she said and pushed through the crowd.

"No thanks." I snorted. *Not likely.* I hung back, warily watching my best friend's ambitions expand to the point that I wondered if they would eclipse our friendship.

With nothing but a bad feeling to keep me company, I scanned the people by me until I found Tucker O'Brian. He was a wrestler who also happened to be on the debate team, so I gave him a free pass on my dumb jock stereotype because of that.

"Hey, Sky." Tucker one-arm hugged me then tipped a flask to his lips.

"Tucker." I took the flask when he handed it to me, relishing the burn of whatever I shot back. "What was that?"

"Tequila." He grinned then tapped the spot on my neck where it met my shoulder. "Got any salt and limes? We could do body shots."

"Hilarious. I'll just pull them out of my purse." I shrugged off his arm.

"You came alone?" He turned for a second then fist-bumped another guy who dropped into his group.

"Nah. Gia's over there." I pointed to where she hung on the outskirts of Damon's crowd.

Desperation washed off her in waves, noticeable even from where I stood, and I hated that look on my best friend. I threw back another shot-sized gulp then handed back Tucker's flask.

Tucker glared in the direction of Gia and the others she stood with. "I can't figure out what's going on with her. I didn't think Gia was like that."

"Like what?"

He pursed his lips, seeming to weigh his words. "I used to think she was sweet, kind. But I don't know. She's changed."

Hasn't she though? He didn't know the how or why, but he saw the results. The way she let the fangirls who hung around the Elite influence her. How fake she acted when the situation called for her to fit in. I didn't like it, either, but I knew what she was made of, and that wasn't it. I suspected the change would be temporary. Gia was good down to her toes. She just hated confrontation.

"She's still the same person, just going through something."

"Hmm." He didn't sound convinced, and he visually tracked her for a few more minutes. "And you're okay with her new friends?"

I snorted. "As if. But whatever. I don't think it'll last. Besides, I have friends like you, so it's not like I'm hiding in a corner while she's with another group of people."

He barked a laugh. "True. That would never be you, Sky."

A wave of excitement swept through the crowd, a charged energy that was impossible to miss. I knew what that meant. One of the Elite would be entering the ring soon.

"Hey, when are you covering a wrestling meet?" His grin widened. "I've been winning all my matches."

"Not my call, Tuck. Stephanie tells us what we're covering." I made a face to show my extreme distaste. "She almost put me on baseball, but I threatened to walk."

His hands found his hips, and he dipped his head for a quiet laugh. He probably had friends on the team and couldn't say anything bad. I didn't care. Baseball made my skin crawl. I hated it with every fiber of my being.

"Is that how you got assigned to cover the football games?"

I rolled my eyes. "Yes. Pure evil on her part."

"Or genius manipulation."

"Or that." I waved away another sip from his flask and studied him, my mind circling back to how he'd looked at Gia. "Why did you ask about Gia? You like her or something?"

He shrugged his big shoulders. "What's not to like? Other than the company she's kept lately."

"Hmm." I filed that away. I wish I'd thought of him when she was looking for a guy to fulfill all her wildest senior dreams. He might not have been able to swing the prom queen one, but that was a long shot no matter what. She would have had a real relationship with Tucker. Based on what I'd just observed—he liked her.

The problem was that everything could go to shit and blow up in our faces. *If she, by some miracle, opens her eyes and loses the filter she has when it comes to Damon and his ridiculous top-tier popularity, could she and Tucker have a shot at something real?* I hoped so.

"There goes your friend's boy!" Tucker had to shout over the crowd's cheers as Damon entered the Ring.

I didn't know Damon's much larger opponent. He had to be from a different school, which was typical for those events. *Could the guy be in college?* A sliver of worry went through me, but I quickly shoved it aside. I didn't care what happened to him. But I didn't mind checking him out. Nothing wrong with that. He was incredible, all six foot two of sculpted muscle that I wouldn't mind running my hands or tongue over.

The announcer did his thing, then Damon and the other beast—who I'd learned was named Steve—circled each other. Goose bumps peppered my skin at the savage expression Damon wore. He moved fast, his fist extending toward Steve's chin. The guy's head snapped back when Damon made contact. He threw a second punch, but Steve managed to block it. They went back and forth with similar combinations. Some made impact. Others, they blocked. It was brutal and adrenaline inducing.

By round two, the crowd was screaming, and both fighters had cuts. Damon's eye was swollen, and his lip had split. It only added fuel to his determination. I cringed as he hit Steve so hard the guy's head snapped back and he stumbled. It was over in a handful of seconds when Damon followed that hit with another across Steve's chin.

Tense and agitated, I found watching him fight hot. I turned to Tucker, motioning for the flask, and took another long pull, needing the alcohol to numb my overactive mind. It wasn't doing me much good.

When I put the cap back on and extended my arm, Tucker's eyes went wide, and his hand dropped from my waist. *When had he put it there?* I didn't remember him touching me. My reactions were slower. I turned to follow what had spooked Tucker and caught a blur before he went down to the ground.

Holy fuck! Damon straddled him, raining punches on Tucker.

"Stop, you asshole!" I screamed then stepped close to help.

Phoenix grabbed me and shifted me behind him. Next, he and Shane tore Damon away and hauled him back. Horrified, I bent to check on Tucker and, with the help of one of his friends, got him to his feet.

"You need to leave, Sky," Phoenix said close to my ear before they herded a snarling Damon in the opposite direction.

I caught a glimpse of blond hair as Gia fawned over him.

Not once did she look my way, and I hated every second of that. It was like Gia had become someone else.

Fuck it. I didn't need to be told twice. I hit the Uber app on my phone and ordered a ride, deciding that helping Tucker after Damon's bullshit beatdown took precedence over saving money for Mom's birthday. By the time I had pushed through the crowd with Tucker and his friend and we got outside, one had arrived. I thanked Tucker's friend, who departed, and helped Tucker get in before following him into the car.

My heart beat a thousand miles a minute. *What was that?* The savage fury on Damon's face and the explosive violence had shocked me to my core. *Over what?* I couldn't make total sense of it.

"I know I have a pack of tissues in here somewhere." I rummaged through my purse as Tucker told the driver his address. "Aha." My trembling fingers closed around the travel package of Kleenexes, and I pulled a few out for him.

Tucker shoved one in his nose to stop the bleeding. The other went to his split lip, then his head fell back against the seat. "You didn't tell me you were dating Damon."

"What? Are you crazy? Why would I date that idiot?"

Tucker rolled his head in my direction so he could pin me with a stern look. "Sky, the guy attacked me for having my hand on your waist. Something's going on."

"Please." I snorted, feigning disgust when in truth, sheer panic chased away the buzz I'd had earlier. "I am not dating that guy."

"Well, then screwing around with him?"

Nope. Not going there. Not analyzing what he said. Just ignoring it all.

The driver pulled up in front of Tucker's house, and Tucker lumbered out of the car.

He grabbed the roof and bent to look back into the vehicle, a resigned smirk curving his bruised and bloody mouth. "Trust me, Sky. Even if something isn't going on at your end, it is on his." He pushed off the car then gave me a small wave. "Later, and thanks for the assist." He winked his good eye—the other was already swelling shut.

After he was inside his house, I told the driver my address. My phone pinged, and I glanced at it, hoping it was Gia apologizing for deserting me. Of course, it wasn't.

Damon: *Are you fucking him?*

What an asshole. I was furious and refused to answer. He sent multiple messages, asking pretty much the same thing. *And if I am, how is that his business?* It wasn't.

When I didn't answer his slew of texts, he switched to calling. I ignored everything until I got home. Mom was asleep, and I tiptoed through the house to get to my room. After shutting the door, I whipped out my phone. Another stupid message came through, asking if I was home.

Me: *I'm in bed*

Which was where I wanted to be. I shimmied out of my jeans and kicked them toward the laundry basket. Then I washed my face, brushed my teeth, and put on pajamas before checking my phone again. Of course, another demanding message waited from him.

Damon: *Prove it*

I snapped a picture of my middle finger in the center of my room with a little message to accentuate how I felt about him. *There's your proof, douchebag.*

Damon: *Do I need to call Gia for a picture?*

I dropped my phone and covered my face with my hands, groaning. *I'm so screwed.* Gia would find out, and I would be done for. I had to stop that from happening before it was too late.

A light tap sounded on my window pane. For fuck's sake. I climbed off my bed and yanked open the blinds. Damon stood outside my window, and I took a resigned breath before unlocking it. He could figure out how to push the window up if he wanted in. I wasn't helping.

Somehow, he popped the screen and set it on the ground, then put his palms flat on the pane and pushed upward until he could fit his hands in and raise it all the way. He pulled himself up with that incredible body strength and was inside way too fast.

"You're taking creepy stalker to a whole new level," I whisper yelled.

Anger crackled around him, which was fine with me. I was beyond mad too.

"What the fuck were you doing with Tucker?" He sat on my bed, way too close.

Butterfly Band-Aids held together the gash over his eye, and I had to curl my fingers to keep from touching him. "Tucker is a friend, jackass. Unlike you."

"He had his hands on you." His blue eyes were stormy, sizzling with heat.

A part of me was so intrigued by his reaction. He was all grrr and possessive, which was strangely a turn-on. It had to be a result of watching him fight in the Ring—not hitting my friend, though.

"That was a dick move on your part. Tucker and I aren't anything but friends. Never have been and never will be. And big deal if he had his arm around me. It was crowded in there. I won't say no to a buffer from being bumped into."

"Yeah, Sky. You are going to tell every guy no, except me. Your lips, hands, and every part of you belongs to me."

I opened my mouth to tell him off, but he was on me before I could breathe a word. His mouth devoured mine hungrily, with an intensity that had my body softening. And suddenly, I wasn't sure I minded how possessive he was.

Which made what we were doing dangerous territory, and I had to stop it. But then he trailed kisses down my neck, throat, jaw, and back to my mouth. My head swam from how incredible he made me feel, and I clung to his broad shoulders.

He slid his hand under my shirt, and at the first skin contact, a sliver of reality pierced my lust-infused brain. I shoved at him. Not because I didn't want him. I did. So much. But I wouldn't do that to Gia.

"Get out."

He pulled back, his eyes scanning every inch of my face, then —by some small miracle—he left the same way he came in. And it took everything I had not to call him back.

CHAPTER TWENTY-FIVE

DAMON

#OVERIT

When my phone rang again—for the thousandth time—I resisted hurling it at the wall and, instead, silenced it. Gia would not take a hint, and I wasn't in the mood to play prince charming right then. I was sore and tired from the fight last night and had a raging hard-on from thinking about Skylar and her luscious mouth. How she'd looked in her room, half-dressed and kiss-drunk, when she'd told me to leave was permanently fixed in my mind.

Her car still sat in the parking lot for Chicks-N-Wings. I needed to get that handled. Shane had the most experience with cars, so I hit his contact button and waited for him to answer.

"What's up?"

"I need to fix Skylar's car or get it to a repair place. Can you check it out with me in an hour?"

"Nah, cuz. I'm supposed to get Tracey from her house in a half hour. We're going to the movies, which is weird as fuck."

"Yeah, that's strange. I don't get it either. Didn't you suggest Netflix or one of the other streaming stations?"

"Yup. She wants me to take her out and for dinner too." He sighed. "I can't help you later, but I have some time now if that works."

"It does."

"I'll be there in a minute. It'll probably be easier if we go together. You can drive her car to her house."

"Sounds good." So much for relaxing. But I needed to get her car done. Shane didn't take long to arrive, and I hopped in his SUV as soon as he pulled into my drive.

"What's the deal with her car?" Shane asked.

"I don't know. She called from work and said that it wouldn't start. She was pissed, so she didn't go into detail."

Shane took his eyes off the road for a minute, his brows furrowing, before he refocused on where we were going. "Do you think someone tampered with it? Jessica is furious about whatever's going on with Gia, and she and Sky are best friends. It makes her fair game."

"Jess would be stupid to do something like that. Gia isn't a threat to the nonexistent relationship she and I have."

"It's not as black and white as you're making it, D."

None of that sounded like him, and I frowned. "This is coming from Tracey?"

"Mostly," he admitted. "You know she wants you and Jess to be official. And Jess is the one you go to most often. Everyone else is a one-nighter."

"And why does what Tracey wants concern me?"

Silence hung between us for an awkward second.

"It doesn't. I'm just relaying information."

"Look, I know you have your reasons for being with Tracey for as long as you have. But her opinion isn't important to me, nor is her friend's. They're not who I would see myself with if I ever wanted to get into a relationship. Which I don't. But one thing you might want to consider is that your twin, the person closest to you in the world, doesn't get along with her. What does that tell you about Tracey?"

Shane pulled into the parking lot, a muscle in his jaw jumping. I probably shouldn't have said what I did, but he should have kept Tracey's opinion out of my life.

"I'm sorry I went there." I smacked him on the shoulder before getting out. He didn't need my opinion on who he chose to date, either, especially with what I was doing with Gia and Sky.

Shane went around to the back of his SUV and retrieved a toolbox while I unlocked Sky's car and popped the hood.

"Try to start the car," Shane instructed.

I got in and turned the key in the ignition. A clicking sound followed but nothing else.

"It sounds like it's the battery."

I grunted and got back into the SUV so we could go pick one up. It would be easy to change, something we both did in shop class. If I'd known that was all it was, I could have managed that myself, but Shane had taken an extra class in mechanics that could have come in handy.

We were back at Sky's car, replacing the battery ten minutes later, when Shane responded about Tracey. "I know Phoenix doesn't like her, and yes, it bothers me. But Tracey was there for me when I needed her. It goes a long way. I don't expect anyone to understand. She has her faults, but I see a lot of good there too."

"I shouldn't have said anything."

He shrugged then attached and tightened the positive and negative cables to the new battery.

"Cole showed me his first-year costs with and without the scholarship he got. Did he send it to you and Phoenix?"

"Yeah. It was an eye-opener. Phoenix's scholarship covers almost everything."

"But not ours." I grinned.

Cole and Phoenix were the stars. They took everything about football seriously. They lived and breathed it. Shane and I loved the game, but it wasn't our be-all and end-all, even if we didn't discuss it openly. The number of times we blew off the runs our brothers did said enough.

"I talked to Granddad about it the other day." Shane returned the screwdriver and wrench to his toolbox and shut the lid. "He covered a majority of the academy's cost to help Mom, though she didn't want to accept it. But college is another story, and he hinted at how proud he was that we were making our way by getting scholarships and figuring things out."

Which meant Shane probably needed even more money than Phoenix. I was glad we'd kept the underground fights going. It was good money and would go a long way to help him manage the upcoming bills. "You got the 'builds character' speech?"

"Yep."

I sensed he didn't want to go too deep into what was expected of him. College was stressful enough with how big of a change it would be. "Aunt Cece is stubborn. Remember when Dad bought you guys the SUVs like ours?"

Dad had bought all four of us identical Range Rovers when we'd gotten our licenses. Shane's mom had had a fit about it, saying she could have bought her sons used cars and didn't need or want anyone to do her job for her.

Shane laughed. "Yeah, she was furious for a few days until she realized we needed a new air conditioner. Then she thanked Uncle Lucas."

"She still made you guys do lawn care for six months to show appreciation."

"The best part"—Shane smirked—"was when your dad gave the gardener paid time off and made you and Cole join us."

The humor fell from his face, and I got the serious side of him, which I didn't want. I knew what was coming.

"That was when you still liked your dad. He made a mistake." He held up his hand when I opened my mouth to tell him to fuck off. "It was a massive one and not without tragic consequence, but he's human. When will you forgive him?"

I was pissed, and I knew my unleashed violence would translate into my tone. "You didn't appreciate that I pushed about Tracey. Same goes for this. Drop it."

Shane shook his head. "Yeah, I don't know why I went there. This conversation is way too heavy for fixing a car." He motioned for me to get in. "See if it starts now."

I sat in Sky's car and twisted the key in the ignition. The engine caught, and I grinned at Shane. "Thanks. Mind following me to drop it off at her house?"

"Let's go." Shane returned the toolbox to the back of the SUV.

I adjusted her seat and mirror while Shane got in his car to follow me.

As soon as he was ready, I pulled out of the parking lot, smiling at the indie rock station she had cued to play on the radio. The car smelled like her—vanilla with a hint of coconut. Oversized black sunglasses sat haphazardly in the console, and the tiny apron she sometimes wore for work lay on the passenger seat. Besides those few things, her car was spotless, which fit her overachieving, organized personality.

It didn't take long before I turned into Sky's driveway. After getting out, I locked up and hid the key on her rear passenger-side tire. Then, I got in Shane's car, which idled at the curb, and texted Sky that it was there and where I'd put the key.

I kept the text simple, leaving out the details of what was wrong. It was fixed, and she would have a way to get places again, which was all that mattered.

Shane drove to my house, and when he pulled into the driveway, I turned to him, my hand on the door handle. "Thanks for your help, and have fun on your date." I couldn't help the grin. We both preferred to stream movies.

"Later," Shane said as I got out and went inside.

I didn't expect Sky to say anything about fixing and delivering her car, but making sure she had it back and that it worked was enough for me.

Not in the mood to do much, I went straight to the basement and got lost in video games for an hour. I needed to decompress from how out of control I felt over anything to do with Sky.

When my stomach growled, I got off the couch and went upstairs. The house was quiet, and I wandered into the kitchen for a snack. The shocked gasp from the kitchen table only annoyed me, and I turned to glare at Raelyn. With her hair dyed back to its original dark brown, she looked so much like Riley.

But she wasn't. In my mind, she was still the enemy.

What she and Dad did to my mom wasn't something I could just get over, like Cole had. Sure, Dad had helped Riley and Raelyn with their horrible situation, but that didn't erase how they'd slept together while he was married to Mom, causing her immeasurable unhappiness. That was something I had been blind to, while Cole had known about him cheating, just not with whom, all along.

"What happened to your face?" Raelyn was out of her chair and headed toward me, her hand raised as if to touch my face.

I jerked back and snapped, "It's none of your business." Then I turned and left the room. I didn't need something to eat that bad. And with how big the house was, I didn't need to run into her. There should be enough space to never see her.

Could this day get any worse? Back in my room, my phone buzzed, and I glanced at it. I shouldn't have tempted the fucking fates because, of course, the day could.

Sky: *You're breaking the agreement—you missed breakfast w/Gia and now you're ignoring her calls*

Me: *She calls a thousand times a day. It's excessive*

Sky: *I don't care. She's upset. Fix it!*

I should never have agreed to Skylar's deal. Not to dating Princess Clingy anyway. Sky's part wasn't so bad. Fuck, her part was incredible. I could go for more of that.

"Damon."

Dad's stern voice effectively shut down my fantasy about Skylar. "What?"

"Go and apologize to Raelyn. She doesn't need, or deserve, your piss-poor attitude."

He filled the doorway, just as tall as me but leaner like Cole. It didn't make him any less intimidating, and the courtroom reacted and bowed down when he was in it. I got off the bed, shouldered past him, and headed for the kitchen.

Raelyn sat curled on the window seat, a book in hand.

When I stomped in, Dad not far behind, I sneered and issued a bullshit apology. "Sorry for snapping at you, but please mind your own business."

I immediately went to the garage and my SUV to escape what my dad would do for that one. I wasn't in the mood for a lecture or whatever ridiculous punishment he planned to enact.

I drove to the field to run drills and work off some of the frustration from the Gia and Skylar situation—and my dad and Raelyn. But when I got there, the marching band was practicing. It was Sunday, and I had no idea if that was typical or a one-off thing.

Instead, I drove past Chicks-N-Wings on the off chance Sky's car was there. It was, so I parked and went in. It wasn't hard to spot her waiting on a table that only Gia occupied. Fuck my life, but it was as good as any a time to handle the situation.

With a fake smile pasted on my mouth, I walked to Gia's table like I was there for her. Skylar approached with food, appearing from the corner of my eye, so I took Gia's hand and pulled her to her feet. Then I kissed her like she was Skylar and not the poor substitute that didn't taste or feel like the girl I conjured in my mind. She didn't kiss like her either.

When I broke the kiss, I kept her hand in mine. "I missed you." Then I released her and sat in the booth opposite where she retook her seat. Flustered, for once, she didn't have a thousand things to say, and I enjoyed the silence.

Gia's cheeks reddened as she continued to sit there, stunned. I flashed a smile while Skylar glared from behind her. When she motioned for me to go to the bathroom, I excused myself from a still-mute Gia.

In the bathroom hallway, I closed the distance to Sky while her eyes flashed with too many emotions. Crowding her against the wall, I leaned in to kiss her, but she shoved at my chest.

"Gia's starting to fall for you," she snarled, baring her teeth.

I laughed, enjoying every minute of how fired up she was. "Jealous?"

"Go to hell." She crossed her arms over her chest. "I'll go out there right now and blow this whole thing apart."

I smirked. She was bluffing. "You won't."

She didn't expect it that time when I slanted my mouth over hers and groaned at how right it felt. When I broke the kiss, too early but necessary, I gave her the reason why she wouldn't do as she'd threatened.

"You won't because you don't want this to end." *And dammit, neither do I.*

CHAPTER TWENTY-SIX

SKYLAR

#CloseCall

Damon didn't stay long, leaving a starstruck Gia to wait for my shift to finish.

The end of my shift couldn't come soon enough, and when I got off, I dragged her to my car. "Let's go back to my house."

"Sure."

Her voice retained that dreamy quality from earlier, and it grated on my nerves.

When we walked into the living room, Mom was seated at the island with a cup of coffee. It was her day off, and she was enjoying a pajama day with no makeup or hair styling.

"Hey, girls." She smiled. "It's so good to see you here, Gia. It feels like forever since you've hung out. Too much rushing around lately."

"Hi, Megan." Gia hugged my mom and fell onto one of the peninsula stools next to her.

My job was a point of contention between Mom and me, but I only needed it for another week or two. I wasn't that into it anyway. Waitressing wasn't my thing, something I'd figured out after the first day—and not because of Damon and his ridiculous demands.

"Gia hasn't been around because she has a boyfriend."

I grabbed two sodas and passed one to Gia, brows raised at Mom. She shook her head no, so I took mine and popped it open, relishing the first sip. It was always the best part of drinking soda.

"That's great news, Gia. It's nice that you girls both have boyfriends." Mom tucked her dark hair behind her ear and took another sip of coffee while Gia's wide Bambi eyes fixated on me. I froze, my drink halfway to my mouth. "Sky spent all night talking to him on the phone, and I found them asleep in his car another time." She fought a smile, enjoying teasing me.

I didn't enjoy it at all and watched Gia to see how she would react. *Would she guess who I was with was Damon?*

Gia smiled and nudged Mom's shoulder before locking me in her sights again. "I want details."

"Um, no." And ew, I wouldn't give my mom details no matter how close we were. It felt a little unsettling. Probably because I was going behind everyone's back and it was wrong. *Then why can't I stop?*

Fortunately, Mom seemed to get the hint and changed the subject. "Gia," she gushed, "I can't get over your transformation. I mean... wow!"

"Senior year." Gia smiled, running a hand over her shorn, dyed hair. "And so far, it's a good one."

Mom and Gia chatted while I stared at them, trying to mask my absolute horror over my situation. My phone buzzed, and I picked it up to find a text from Damon. He said something about checking off number three in my four-point plan. *Not my phone.*

It was Gia's, and number three was about losing her v-card. I set it down quickly as Mom excused herself to answer a call about scheduling an appointment. I scooted the phone over to Gia, and after she read the text, she hugged it to her chest, then jumped off the stool and did a little dance.

Afterward, she handed me the phone, but I'd already read the message. I couldn't tell if I was jealous or worried—or both.

Thank God Mom was in the other room. I couldn't let Gia go through with it. "Hey, don't you think things are moving a little fast?"

"Yeah." She bounced on her feet, nervous excitement spilling from her in waves. "He hasn't even tried for second base, but this is what I want."

"I think you should wait. Damon… he's not the guy you think he is, and this is a big deal."

Gia huffed. "Stop worrying. I love Damon, and eventually—probably after tonight—he'll love me too. Besides"—that sly grin was back, and I didn't like it—"I've been researching."

I was going to regret asking. "Researching how?"

She shrugged like she was all worldly. "Books and some movies."

"Porn?" It felt like my eyes might pop out of my head. I couldn't imagine her doing that.

Gia's face turned beet red. "You shouldn't be jealous." She changed the subject. "It'll happen for you too. Maybe with Tucker."

Because that was who she thought I was on the phone and asleep in the car with. Part of me was relieved.

"I saw you with him at the fight. Why didn't you tell me that you guys were dating?" She nibbled her lower lip as I stood across from her, too stunned to speak. "I used to have a major crush on Tucker in eighth grade. Maybe we can compare notes when it happens for you too."

"Uh, sure." *No. Absolutely not.* I wouldn't sleep with Tucker.

He wasn't my type. He was a great guy, and I liked him as a friend, but no. He wasn't *that* guy. Damon was totally *that* guy, and I hated myself for it. But that wasn't why I didn't want Gia to have sex with him.

When Gia left, I sent Damon a text—*we need to talk.*

CHAPTER TWENTY-SEVEN

DAMON

\#Promises

When Sky texted me to meet her at the park near her house, I almost broke the sound barrier driving there. She parked her car in the same spot I had the past two times we were there. When I pulled into the space next to hers and turned off the engine, she hopped out of her car and yanked open my passenger-side door.

The wind whipped her long hair around her head, and she had to lean close to me to keep it out of the way as she shut the door. The full moon and streetlamp were our only sources of light.

I didn't have to wait for her to air her grievances with the stunt I'd pulled with Gia. She jumped all over me, and what a gorgeous sight. Sky mad was like a raging storm of the darkest kind, and I loved every minute of it.

"If you sleep with Gia, everything between us is finished." Her blue eyes darkened with emotion. "I'll tell Gia myself."

I smirked, unable to resist stirring the pot. "No need to be jealous. There's enough of me to go around."

Red stained her cheeks. "No. And gross."

It was hard not to laugh because Sky didn't like sharing. I doubted she would admit it to herself, but I'd caught the look on her face after I'd kissed Gia. She didn't like it. Not at all. "I'm getting laid one way or another. You can let your friend have what she wants, or I can 'cheat' on her. Unless… you're volunteering to take Gia's place."

The wind howled against the car, and trees bent in the distance, a mere silhouette to the moon's bright glow.

"What?"

Sky's features betrayed nothing, but her voice held the dark storm in her mind, and I wanted to experience her barely contained wildness.

"Gia's ready to take things to the next level, and I'm tired of the forced celibacy. Everybody thinks she's my girlfriend because that's what she's saying. I can call this whole thing off right now and tell Gia that her friend has been taking matters into her own hands. Then you can deal with that among yourselves."

She shook her head, her hair dancing around her shoulders. "You're a dick."

I wanted to kiss her dirty mouth, to touch her, but I didn't want to say all that and look desperate. "Gia's the one who wants it. But if it's any consolation, I would rather have sex with you." I waited for her to rip me a new one or, at the very least, to tell me to screw myself.

"Okay. Fine."

I sat there for a moment, almost offended by her attitude. "Chicks want me. Your *friend* wants me. But you're acting like fucking me is a punishment."

"I'm not one of your groupies." She crossed her arms over her chest and glared.

"I'll need a certain level of enthusiasm."

Her upper lip curled. "Enthusiasm is earned."

I smirked. *Oh yeah, I love a good challenge.* We were locked in a stare off. It was fucking crazy. Sky wasn't my type—she hated sports and me. Her friend wasn't my type, either, but Sky was like an addiction. And I wanted her. I moved the console back and grabbed her hips to lift her onto me, but she smacked my hands away.

"I'm not doing this in your truck."

"Fine. Come over Thursday night." My dad and Raelyn had a client dinner and would be in the city for the weekend. It would be the perfect time.

"If I do this"—she was eerily still, her features intense as she delivered her message—"you have to promise not to screw Gia."

I shrugged. I didn't want to sleep with that chick anyway. "I'll promise so long as you don't stand me up or back out."

"Okay, fine. I promise."

When she turned to get out, I put my hand on her shoulder, and she swiveled back with a question in her deep-blue eyes. Then I kissed her. Not like how I usually did but soft and slow, savoring the feel of her. I took my time and felt the kiss all the way to my gut.

When I released her, she popped open the door, her grip on it tight so the wind wouldn't take it. Then she was gone, sliding into her car. The engine started. She backed up and was out of there before I moved to hit the Start button on mine. On the drive home, I realized I looked forward to a night with her much more than I wanted to admit.

And because of that, the week went by slowly. I saw Gia every day, but not Sky, though I texted her a countdown every morning. She didn't respond to me until Thursday, when she asked what time she should come over.

I wanted her to drop everything and come immediately, but I told her eight and to dress in something sexy.

CHAPTER TWENTY-EIGHT

SKYLAR

#BuhbyeVCard

My hands shook as I flipped through the clothes in my closet. Frustrated and even a little scared, I flopped onto my bed, unsure of what to do about Damon's request —*order, command, dictate?* I didn't own sexy clothes. I had shorts, T-shirts, jeans, and a couple of sweaters. My bras and panties didn't even match. *Should they match?*

I stared at my ceiling as time ticked by way too fast. I had to come up with something that worked for that night. Phone in hand, I called Gia because, if anyone knew what to wear in my situation, it would be her. It rang several times then rolled into voicemail, and I hung up. *Where is she?* I pushed out a breath, rolled over to my pillow, shoved my face in it, and screamed. I had to go to the mall and figure it out.

With my purse in hand, I hurried to my car, stressed and annoyed that I was even thinking of spending money on some-thing Damon wanted. But it wasn't just that. I was incredibly nervous. Maybe shopping would help. I had no clue. I needed to talk to Gia.

I blasted music and did everything I could to stop panicking as I drove to the mall. When that didn't work, I made mental lists. *Get a matching set of bra and panties. Black.* I was most comfortable in that color. *And then what? A dress?* That seemed extreme.

At the mall, I speed-walked to a well-known lingerie store. I was about to go in when a bubbly laugh caught my attention. I turned and spotted Gia with several cheerleaders who hung around the Elite, minus Jessica and Tracey—the leaders of that unpleasant group. I was surprised Gia had moved up the social ladder so quickly and that she would associate with those girls. The few she was with were catty, not as nasty as the other two, but they would get there.

If I stayed where I was, they would walk right by me, and I couldn't move if I wanted to. She hadn't answered my call, and I saw why.

They neared, and her gaze locked onto mine before she tore her eyes away as she passed without saying a word. My hand flattened against the display window, and I worked to control my emotions. She'd ignored me, after all I'd done for her. Anger took the place of hurt. Fuck it. I whirled and returned to my car without buying anything. I would wear what I had on, and he would like it or not. I didn't care.

I'd been to a party at Damon's before and didn't need to plug his address into the GPS. When I got to his huge house, I parked around the corner and walked—no need to give anyone a reason to gossip. And if Gia stopped by unexpectedly, she wouldn't see my car. It killed me, but I cared about hurting her, no matter how she'd behaved at the mall.

Damon's oceanfront house had an incredible view. I couldn't imagine a life like that, not that I was jealous. I was happy with what Mom and I had—each other. After what we'd gone through, that was everything.

I couldn't bring myself to open the car door, so I sat there for a hot minute, sorting through my feelings. It was stupid. Everything about me being there was. But I couldn't ignore how I needed him to know that having sex was new for me.

Cass, a friend at school who'd graduated with Riley and Cole's class, had told me once when she'd slept with Damon that it was "back-against-the-wall, all-consuming, you'll-never-forget-it kind of sex." I couldn't lie and say it didn't intrigue me —it did. She and Damon hadn't lasted. It was a one-time thing, according to her. *And isn't that his usual MO?* Besides, she'd had her sights set on Matt Chambers, and they were happily dating at Thane, last I'd heard.

But that comment had stayed with me, and while I wanted to experience that—it *was* my first time. I wasn't sure how well I would do with his aggressiveness when I was so nervous. *Gah, get a grip. It's not that big of a deal.*

Or, I didn't think it was for me. Gia was a different story. She needed romance and love. I wasn't sure I had the same needs. Maybe, but there was no point in examining them closer —I was doing it.

My mind skipped back to when Gia had first told me about her senior year goal list, *"Number three, lose my v-card."* My reaction had been more like me than how I was behaving currently —*"Oh my God, Gia. It's not like it's a disease."* Yet, there I was, overthinking everything.

My head thumped against my headrest, and I pushed out a slow breath. *Stop procrastinating.* I grabbed my phone, hit the button to call Damon, and set it on speaker. Each ring screaming through the speaker added another layer to my frayed nerves. Then he answered, and my entire body tensed.

"Ticktock, Sky."

Though he couldn't see me, I rolled my eyes and felt a fraction better from the gesture. "I'm aware. And I'm nearby." My leg bounced, and I gripped my thigh to stop the nervous tic.

"You're not chickening out, are you?"

"No." My teeth sank into my bottom lip. *Why am I so nervous?*

"Then what's stopping you?"

His voice changed, but I couldn't put my finger on how. It sounded softer, more patient. Regardless of what that meant, I responded to it.

"I need to talk to you about… things before I go inside your house." Because once there, I wasn't sure I would have the nerve. That would be unlike me, but the whole situation was strange. It made me feel so vulnerable, which I hated, and Damon was a master at exposing me.

"I'm listening."

"I know how you are. Girls talk." That didn't sound like how I'd meant it. I banged my head a few times against the headrest, silently cursing under my breath.

"Why are you listening to other people? That's not your style, McCormick."

I snapped out of my anxiety-driven mood at the sound of my last name. It gave me the space to pull back and state the problem without getting too into my head. "I've never slept with anyone before. I felt like you needed to know that."

"Thanks for telling me."

He kept his voice level and low, a whisper of a caress in it that I immediately responded to by tightening my thighs.

"Mm-hmm."

"We don't have to do this, you know. Or we can go as far as you want."

"No. I'm… I don't have an attachment to my v-card like some people." *Gia.* "It is what it is. An experience. Not a huge rite of passage and a memory I'll always hold onto. At least it doesn't feel like that."

"Are you sure about that? I won't take something from you

that you're not ready to give. I promise. Don't feel pressure from me to go all the way. That wouldn't be fair."

He was acting awfully human, which threw me for a loop. "Where's all the posturing? The threats? This isn't like you."

He chuckled, and the sound danced over my skin. I didn't know how much longer I wanted to stay in the car and talk. It made me feel even more exposed. I should have made a mic-drop announcement, hung up, stomped to his front door, and said, *Let's do this.* That was more my style. Our current conversation was something else entirely.

"I want you to be sure. No crying foul later."

"Dick." But I smiled. It felt good to tell him. "Better make it good. I have high expectations, and you have a reputation to uphold." What Cass had said rolled through my mind again, not for the first time. *What will that be like?* I wanted to experience it. A rush of heat swept through me at the thrill of seeing him naked. His body was a work of art, and I salivated to get my hands on all of him.

"Don't you worry about a thing. Just give me five minutes, okay?"

"Sure." *What for?* I wanted to ask, but I wouldn't. *What if he's pulling a first-date prep thing like Ben Stiller did in* There's Something About Mary? *Nope. No thanks.* I would keep my questions to myself.

We hung up, and I messed around with the radio, searching for anything to distract me from what I was doing. Because I had no idea what that was. My gaze darted to the dash to check the time too often, so I set a timer on my phone for six minutes. I didn't want to appear too eager, or too late. The stakes were set, and I planned to follow through with them.

I went to my emails and responded to a few from Stephanie. She liked my articles much better than the first one I'd published without her approval at the start of the year.

I grinned at the thought of the article where I'd slammed Damon. He'd been so pissed.

The alarm went off, blaring like a thousand horns, and I almost jumped out of my skin. I couldn't press the off button fast enough and missed the first two times. *Get a grip!* My hands were instantly sweaty, and I rubbed them on my shorts.

Before I could change my mind, I jabbed the doorbell with my finger. If I thought about what I was doing, I would panic. The door opened before I fully spiraled. Damon filled the doorway with his broad shoulders and height. Not that I was short, but he was big. *Shit.* I needed to turn off my brain.

Then he reached out and grabbed my hand. Leading me inside, he took me past the marble foyer with the gigantic crystal chandelier, through the stunning gourmet kitchen and family room combo, then up the stairs. We went into a bedroom decorated in grays and blues. Candles adorned every surface, casting a warm, romantic glow.

"Are these for me?" I was surprised and even touched that he'd made such an effort to make me more comfortable. I looked around his room, which could fit both mine and Mom's inside it, and was shocked by how clean it was. I had expected his room to be a sty and suspected that he'd just picked up.

"Of course they are. You deserve to feel special."

I was done for. I wasn't sure I would survive a night with him. He had to stop saying things like that to me. He could shatter me if I didn't try to maintain a wall between us.

Damon moved around me, toward his bed, and pulled out a bottle of vodka from a drawer in his bedside table. "Do you want a drink?"

"No." I just wanted to get it over with. I grabbed the hem of my T-shirt and whipped it over my head. I hadn't changed from the sports bra I'd worn to the mall, and I worried he would laugh at me.

He grinned. "Is all that sexy for me?"

I laughed, feeling a bit more at ease. "It's your favorite. The same one I wore for your bra pic request."

"Ah, I thought I recognized it." His blue eyes danced with mirth. "Definitely a favorite memory. And if you wouldn't come after me with a pitchfork over it, that would make a tempting screensaver."

"Maybe not a pitchfork, but a bat would be a given." I winked.

He closed the distance between us, his expression changing from amused to heated as his eyes dilated. When he placed a hand on my hip, my stomach tensed. He traced a finger along the bottom edge of my sports bra just beneath my breasts.

"You're beautiful. It doesn't matter what you wear."

When he bent and teasingly brushed his lips over mine, I wrapped my arms around his neck. In his embrace, I felt sexy and wanted. Tangling my fingers in his hair, I tugged, and he deepened the kiss. *Yes.* I loved how he kissed. It was incredible, and I barely registered when he guided me to the edge of his giant bed.

He broke the kiss briefly to pull his shirt over his head in that sexy way guys did by grabbing the back of it behind their head. He tossed it to the floor before he eased my arms up and peeled off my sports bra. My breath quickened. I didn't have huge breasts like Gia. I was average at best, and it made me self-conscious.

"Fuck, Sky." Damon's eyes burned a trail over my body.

Fuck what? Does he regret this? I tried to pull away, my sights set on where my shirt had landed.

"What are you doing?"

I shrugged. "I just…" I glanced at the ceiling, trying to get control of my turmoil inside.

"You're beautiful. Don't doubt that for a second."

Air whooshed out of me, and I returned my hands to his perfect body, sliding them over his chiseled muscles until my arms wrapped around the back of his neck. I played with the ends of his thick, dark hair. He pulled me close, and I gasped at the skin-to-skin contact. Then his mouth was on mine. I parted on a moan, losing myself in the kiss. A thread of urgency in how he devoured me replaced the tenderness from before, and I shivered in response.

But when his hands didn't move from my hips, a seed of doubt injected into my foggy brain. I pulled away enough to break the kiss. I hated how insecure I was, but it was new, and he hadn't moved his hands, like at all. *What does that mean?*

It bothered me. "Did you change your mind?"

"No. Why? Are you trying to get out of having sex with me?"

I shook my head and meant it, surprising even me. "No. I just didn't know you wanted to go slow."

A growl left his mouth, and I sucked in a gasp before he was on me. His mouth slanted over mine, and I trembled beneath the sensual onslaught. Goose bumps followed in the wake of his hand as he trailed it up my side then cupped my breast, teasing and rolling my nipple. I pushed into him, eager for more.

His lips left mine, trailed open kisses down my neck and over the top of my breasts, then took my other nipple in his mouth. I arched into him. His hands grabbed my ass, and I wrapped my legs around his waist as he lifted me. My breasts felt swollen, heavy, and ached for more.

He lowered me onto the bed, where I unwound my legs from his waist. Several seconds passed as he just looked at me. A slow wave of heat swept through my body, and I fought not to squirm. A gentle caress at my hip, then he hooked his finger at the waistband of my cotton shorts. He slid them and my panties down my legs with agonizing slowness until they joined our shirts on the floor. His jeans followed, but he left on the tight black boxer briefs, and some part of me breathed a sigh of relief. I was ready, but I also wasn't.

When he climbed onto the bed and spread my legs, I

resisted, my heart pounding so fast I feared it would make a break for it.

"Stop. What are you doing?" I bit my lower lip, stifling the panic he must have heard.

"Looking at you." He licked his lower lip. "Tasting you."

His hand caressed my thigh, sending heat-seeking missiles to my core. He bent to the inside of my leg, trailing slow kisses while his hands touched every part of my legs. It felt good, and the tension that'd shot through me slowly eased. When he sensed my lack of resistance, his fingers grazed the edges of where I wanted him most, and my eyes drifted shut. I wanted it. I couldn't deny it.

Need made me writhe beneath his touch, and when he grazed my clit, I squirmed, helpless against the wave of sensations. The pad of his thumb circled it. He dipped his finger inside me then spread the wetness over the small bundle of nerves, and I moaned, arching my hips into his touch.

His kisses drew closer, and desire raged through me. All embarrassment was gone as I chased the climax that hovered just out of reach. At the first touch of his mouth, I gasped and tangled my fingers in his hair, urging him to keep going. His tongue was magic as he licked, sucked, and tasted while thrusting a finger deep inside me. Then another joined the first, and I felt full as he stretched me.

Every nerve ending fired faster than before. When he circled my clit and curled his fingers deep inside, I screamed his name, blind to everything but the way my climax exploded through me. Pulsing waves of desire heated every inch of me, momentarily stealing my strength, and I went limp.

When I looked down, Damon's satisfied grin and hooded, lust-filled eyes sent a renewed thrill through me. He slid his fingers out with excruciating slowness, and I whimpered from the loss. They went into his mouth, and he sucked my wetness from them. The sight was incredibly erotic.

His satisfied grin coaxed one from me too. If that hadn't been my first time, I could only imagine what I would do with, and to, him. He stood and practically tore off his boxer briefs. I nibbled on my lower lip as he rolled on a condom. I was worried and excited to feel his long, thick length pushing inside me.

He climbed onto the bed, his biceps flexing as he held still above me. I wrapped my legs around his waist, digging my heels in, urging him to push inside. He chuckled then lowered himself, and I welcomed his weight.

"You sure about this, Sky? No foul if you change your mind."

"Shut up." I tugged his head down and kissed him while lifting my hips. No matter how much I squirmed or what I did, he controlled every inch he fed into me. Fullness as I'd never felt had my core pulsing, and I arched my back, drowning in the feel of him.

He pushed in with one swift thrust, then held still, swallowing my gasp as he deepened the kiss. The pain was fleeting, quickly forgotten. Sensing I was ready, he moved deliciously slow, stoking our desires. My nails bit into his skin as the sensations built, and our kiss ended. The pace changed from slow to fast and desperate.

I restlessly trailed my hands over his shoulders and back, his muscles bunching and flexing beneath my touch. I met him thrust for thrust. I couldn't take my eyes off his intense expression above me, the raw hunger and need etched in his beautiful face, and the wall around my heart fractured.

He slipped a hand between us, circling my swollen nub until I cried out and fell over the edge. My body squeezed his as I came apart in his arms. His control snapped, and he thrust hard and deep until a shudder tore through his body. Then he spilled himself deep in me. Well, the condom, but I felt the powerful pulse all the same. When he collapsed on top of me, I traced the contours of his back and toyed with the soft strands of his hair. I didn't want it to end, but that wasn't our reality.

We didn't lie there long, not nearly enough time. But I had to go and nudged his heavy weight so he would move.

The tenderness he'd shown surprised me and was something I would have to keep me company later when it was over between us.

CHAPTER TWENTY-NINE

DAMON

#STFU

Sky left like her ass was on fire after I got up to dispose of the condom. She'd pulled her clothes on in record time and mumbled something about needing to get home. Not to bother showing her out, either, because she remembered the way. Watching her run from her emotions amused me because they were on display all over her face.

She'd more than liked what we'd done, and a heady dose of satisfaction rushed through me as I lay back on the bed. When my phone rang, I assumed it was her and didn't bother looking at the screen when I answered.

"Hi. What're you doing?" Gia sounded breathless.

"Working out," I lied. "I'll call you later." I ended the call, not even bothered that it'd been her. All I wanted to do was remember every minute with Sky.

It was hard to believe she had been a virgin. She sure as fuck didn't kiss like one. Or respond or touch me like it was her first time. Sure, she'd been nervous, but she had been incredibly sensual. I loved how she felt, tasted, and sounded. And I wanted her again.

I texted her to come back, but she didn't respond. So, finally, I hit the shower. A half-naked girl sat on the edge of my bed when I got out of the shower and wrapped a towel around my waist. Gia wore a button-down shirt, undone to her waist, showing her lacy white bra and breasts that it barely contained. I felt nothing. She had a good body and was pretty, but she wasn't who I wanted. And my dick was in full agreement without even a twitch.

"Perfect timing," she purred. "I just took a shower too." She shimmied her shoulders, shaking her tits.

And I had to admit they were nice. Full and almost spilling out of the bra, but she just didn't do it for me, something I never thought I would think. "I'm not ready for this yet with you. Or anyone." I winked, so full of shit I was surprised she hung on every word I said. "My rep's all hype, and things are moving a little fast between us."

I grabbed my clothes and took them into the bathroom to change. I never used that line in situations like these, but I wanted Sky. And telling her friend to fuck off might upset Sky, something I wasn't willing to do.

I wasn't shy and had never hidden to get dressed when a girl was around, but after sleeping with Sky, it felt wrong. When I came back out, fully clothed, Gia had gotten dressed, and she tugged nervously at the hem of her shirt.

"How'd you get in?" That bothered me.

"The door was unlocked, and when no one answered, I thought I'd take a chance to see if you were inside." She mashed her lips together. "At school, I heard you and Phoenix talking about how your parents were out of town this weekend, and I thought it would be a good time to, you know…"

I let it go. Sky must have left the door unlocked when she'd bailed. "Want to go to the movies?"

"Sure." Gia smiled, her confidence returning with the olive branch.

I took her to a romantic comedy, hoping it would hold her interest more than the action film I would have preferred.

After buying the tickets, I ushered her into the dark theater and to seats, ignoring her nonstop chatter about the actors, movie, or whatever it was I tuned out. We settled into the plush faux-leather recliners, and she fell blessedly silent as the lights dimmed and the previews filled the screen.

I couldn't believe I had to keep the charade going with Gia, even if it was the only way I could get with Sky—which rankled. Gia's cloying floral perfume vied with the vanilla and coconut scent associated with Sky's skin. Each inhalation annoyingly erased Sky's scent and the animallike state of satisfaction that being with her brought.

"That looks good." Gia's hand gripped my forearm.

"Mm-hmm." I had no idea what the preview had been. I preferred the one replaying in my mind in explicit detail. The way Sky had melted against me when I'd kissed her. That breathy moan she made. The softness of her skin. How she never shied away, and that stubborn tilt of her chin when she felt challenged.

Head resting on the headrest, I let my eyes drift shut as the movie finally started. I wanted Sky again—once was not nearly enough. That aggravating part of my mind whispered cruelly that the only way to her was through faking it with Gia. I was coming to hate that more and more.

Gia's head rested on my shoulder, and my body tensed.

"I'm going to get us some snacks." I stood, dislodging her, and stepped into the aisle.

When I pushed the door open from the theater room to the subdued lights in the hall, I stood there for a minute and decompressed. It wasn't a long movie. Then I could dump Gia back at her house. Besides, it should win me points with Sky, and I was all over that.

I took my time getting two popcorns and drinks so we didn't have to share. It would keep her mouth and hands busy if nothing else. I checked my phone while in the lobby. *Fuck.* Shoving it back in my pants, I cursed how ridiculous I was being. But I couldn't help the need to see Sky's name light the screen.

What is she thinking? Did she like what we did? I snorted. Of course she did. Sky was nothing if not responsive. Besides, she would have told me in graphic detail if she'd hated any part of it.

I grinned. She was fucking fierce in everything she did, and I had no problem admitting how much I liked that about her. I rechecked my phone then attempted to shove all thoughts of Sky from my mind. It wasn't possible, but hey, I tried.

Snacks in hand, I went back in. I handed Gia hers then situated my popcorn on my thigh. I didn't plan on eating it but used it as the prop I'd meant it to be.

"Thanks," she whispered then leaned close. "Did you hear about the party next weekend? Rebecca told me about it. I thought maybe we could go together?"

"Maybe. I'll have to see what's going on." I had a moment of weakness and whispered, "Are you sure about that party? It's not an academy one." Parties outside the academy tended to be rougher, and something about Gia screamed naive. If I didn't take her, it probably wasn't a good idea for her to go. Rebecca hadn't been looking out for her when she'd passed along the information. "If I can't go, you should take Sky with you."

She nodded, her big brown eyes melting with gratitude. "Thanks for looking out for me. You're right. Sky would never let anything happen to either one of us. Of course, I would be safe if you took me."

I wanted to roll my eyes, but I gave her a small smile then

turned my attention back to the screen. Another few minutes passed while she watched the movie and I plotted how to convince Sky to have sex with me again.

Her arm bumped into mine. I shifted away and rechecked my phone—still nothing. Gia's leg pressed against mine. I ground my teeth.

"What do your cousins think of us dating?"

Fuck. "Nothing." *Because we're not dating.*

"Shane and Tracey are going to get married. I just know it. They look so good together." Her finger trailed over my hand. "Do you want to get married someday?"

Is she for real? "No."

"I totally respect you for wanting to wait to have sex."

I shoved a handful of popcorn in my mouth. *Why are we watching this movie if she plans on talking through it?* If I'd known she would, I would have taken her to the action one.

"If we don't go to the party next weekend, we should go on a road trip and visit your brother. I bet the parties at Thane are crazy. I would love to go to one."

"Mm." I was done talking.

She could say whatever she wanted, but my mind was on what had happened earlier, when I'd had access to all of Sky, and I preferred it to stay that way.

My phone vibrated, and I yanked it from my pocket. But it wasn't Sky. Phoenix had sent a group text to his brother and me about working out later. My fingers flew over the screen as I responded to him, then I hit the button on the side to extinguish the bright light, turning the phone back off. I didn't put it in my pocket again.

We made it twenty minutes before her hand rested on my thigh. Halfway into the movie, she slid it higher and tried to stroke my dick. When she leaned into me and whispered that she would jerk me off if I wanted, I removed her hand and told her no, I just wanted to watch the movie.

CHAPTER THIRTY

SKYLAR

#ComingClean

Ahh! I tossed my phone on my bed and flopped backward, bouncing slightly on the mattress. It'd been three days since we'd slept together, and I couldn't get him out of my mind. I didn't want to want Damon, or to check my phone a billion times, hoping he had messaged me. I turned onto my side, curling into a ball.

I didn't want to care if he was out with Gia or at home doing her. But I did. I cared too much. And because I couldn't tell Gia how I felt, I had no one to talk to. It sucked so badly.

Wanting Damon was a losing game.

Rather than lie there in a ball of self-pity, I grabbed the book on my nightstand and tried to read. When I read the same paragraph three times without having any idea what it said, I tossed it aside. I couldn't concentrate. I checked my phone—again. Nothing.

Wandering to the family room, I dropped onto the couch

and turned on the TV. I was home alone, as Mom worked that Sunday since she had it off last week. I wished she were with me. We could have gone and done something. Even waitressing would have helped take my mind off Damon. But of course, I wasn't scheduled.

Annoyed, I grabbed my purse and went outside, deciding to take a walk. It was better than moping around the house. I walked for a long time until I heard the sound of the waves and followed them to the pier.

It was crowded, and I wove through people, feeling marginally better as the sun began its descent. I sidestepped a rather large guy, but his hand shot out and lightly grabbed my arm. I looked up and smiled when I saw who it was.

"Hi, Tucker." He still had a shiner from when Damon had hit him repeatedly. "How's it going?"

"Sky." He grinned then tugged me over to the side of the pier and away from where people were walking. "I wanted to thank you for making sure I got home after the fight."

"Of course." I shook my head. "I can't believe Damon did that to you. How do you feel?"

"I'm fine. Did you ever find out his deal where you're concerned?"

It was dangerous territory. "There's nothing. He's dating my friend Gia. I have no idea why he went out of his mind."

Tucker chuckled. "He may be dating her, but he's into you."

I rolled my eyes, refusing to engage. "What are you doing here?"

"I was hanging out with Trent and Melissa. They left to get homework done, and I don't have any, so…"

"Want to hang out with me at the festival?"

A traveling one had set up not far from there.

"Yeah, sounds good," he agreed.

We walked down the beach, chatting about college applications and majors, where we wanted to go, and how weird living away from home would be. We kept up the easy banter when we got to the fair, and I laughed often. He was the perfect distraction, and if anything had been budding in his mind at the fight with all the touching, it wasn't there anymore. We were just friends, like we'd always been.

The small hairs on the back of my neck rose, and I didn't need to turn from the shooting game I was playing with Tucker to confirm who had arrived.

"Sky!" Gia shrieked as she and Damon stopped beside us.

Tucker finished his shots and set the game gun down, then we both shifted our focus to Gia and Damon. I clenched my teeth, annoyed that she was finally talking to me. Excitement pinkened her cheeks as she looked back and forth between Tucker and me.

"I can't believe we're all here at the same time," she said.

I nodded noncommittedly as Gia kept gushing happily over seeing us. We were quite the foursome. I glanced at Tucker's black eye, and Damon wore his normal scowl. I was unhappy for my own reasons.

Gia was the only one talking, and I wondered how she could be so oblivious. I barely looked her in the eye. Anger built the more she blabbered about the stupid festival. How she'd treated me hurt, and I wasn't coping well.

"How are Tina and Rebecca?" I couldn't help throwing shade.

She had fucking seen me at the mall while she'd been with the sophomore social climbers who hung around Damon and his cousins.

Gia's smile wavered, but she soldiered through, ignoring my question. "We should all go on the Ferris wheel together." She gestured behind her.

"No thanks." I didn't want to stay and watch her and Damon having fun. And not because I would owe him another "favor" but because I didn't like how much I wanted to give him one. I turned and walked away.

Tucker followed. His truck was parked by the pier, and he gave me a ride home, letting me stew in silence. That was one of the reasons I liked him. He could read the room and be okay with letting me deal with things in my way.

By the time I said goodbye, thanked him for the ride, and let myself into the house, I had ten messages from Damon. Some were threats, asking if my mom knew I was the kind of girl who fucked one guy in the afternoon and another in the evening.

It wasn't twice in the same day, douchebag. I'd screwed Damon Thursday and had done nothing with Tucker that Sunday. I wanted to scream at him. But instead, I realized what it all meant. It was time to end things.

I punched my response into the phone, taking my fury out on the innocent buttons. *The deal's off. I'm telling Gia tomorrow.*

CHAPTER THIRTY-ONE

DAMON

#Busted

I should have given Tucker a second black eye to match the one from just over a week ago. *Does he have a death wish, showing up with Sky?* She was mine. And if he hadn't figured that out by how I'd jumped him, he was a lot dumber than I'd thought.

When Sky and Tucker had left, I'd dragged Gia through the crowd to the car then dropped her at home. Once she was inside, I put my SUV in park and went straight to Skylar's house. A light shone in her bedroom window, and I could see her silhouette through the blinds.

I banged on the glass pane since the screen was still in the bushes from when I'd taken it off last time. "Open the window, or I'll fucking break it." I was pissed enough to do it too.

It took her too long to open it, angering me even more. And when she finally did, she backed up, her arms crossed over her chest as she glared at me. I climbed in.

"I can't—"

"Shh," she shushed me, her voice low and heated as she stepped closer to make her point. Anger burned in her eyes, turning them a deep blue.

I lowered my voice to match hers. "I can't believe you fucked me Thursday, and now you're screwing Tucker. The guy's a tool."

"Excuse me? He's a friend. But *if* I were fucking Tucker, it wouldn't be any of your business." A dark grin curved her lips. "Turnabout is fair play. You do that kind of shit all the time. One and done? Ring a bell? We had sex. It was good. And now we're done."

Not happening. I wrapped my arm around her waist and pulled her to me. "We're done when I say we are." It was a bullshit thing to say, but in the heat of the moment, I wasn't very rational.

I didn't let her respond as I slanted my lips over hers with all the heat and desperation I felt. It only took one second for her body to melt into mine, and she returned the kiss.

Need raged between us like a goddammed inferno of desire. I had to have her, and from the way she kissed me back, I knew the feeling was mutual.

I buried my hand in her hair, angling her head to deepen the kiss. Too many clothes stood between us, and I tugged on her shirt with my free hand until she broke the kiss, stepped back, and whipped it over her head.

My grin matched hers as I shed my clothing as fast as she did hers. We stood before each other, naked. She was so goddammed beautiful.

She pushed back the covers, but I had a different idea.

"Hold on." I shoved her pillow to the floor and got on the bed, my back to the headboard. Then I grabbed her by the hips and lifted her so she straddled my legs.

Her hands went to my shoulders, and with desire-glazed

eyes, she traced one of my tattoos down my bicep. I grazed the inside of her thigh with the back of my hand. Her pulse fluttered at the base of her neck, and I pressed a kiss there.

She was so soft. Touching her was heaven, and I would never get enough. "You're so damn sexy."

I trailed my hand along her outer thigh and around her flat stomach. Then I parted her slick folds and teased her sensitive bud. She threw her head back as she moaned. I pumped my fingers in a slow caress, teasing her and making her gasp. I urged her closer, consumed by how much I wanted her.

When she lifted onto her knees, I positioned myself at her entrance and guided her down, our eyes clinging to each other the entire time. It was fucking erotic, and I captured her mouth, devouring her as I rocked her hips on top of me, showing her what to do.

She clung to my shoulders as she rode me, the sight the most incredible thing I'd ever witnessed. Sky was sinfully gorgeous. I increased the tempo as passion built between us. I knew I couldn't take much more—her breathy moans and how her body clenched mine drove me to the point of madness.

I trailed kisses over her neck and breasts, groaning against her skin as she ground against me. When I lifted my gaze to her, I felt a connection like none other. My desire swelled, and I slipped my hand between us to swirl a gentle caress over her sensitive bundle of nerves. Taking her lips in a drugging kiss, I swallowed her scream as she exploded around me, squeezing me like a vise. I increased the tempo of her hips, chasing her climax with one of my own just as the bedroom door swung open.

Gia and Sky's mom stood in the doorway.

The End

Ready to find out what happens between Damon and Skylar? To find out, continue reading the Hidden Valley Elite series with <u>Brutal Nights</u>:
https://www.islavaughnauthor.com/books

Keep up with Isla's releases by joining her newsletter:
https://bit.ly/IslaVaughnNewsletter

If you enjoyed reading Brutal Days as much as I did writing it, I hope you'll consider leaving a review.

ABOUT THE AUTHOR

Isla Vaughn is the author of the Hidden Valley Elite series. Her romance books are full of complex characters, strong alpha males, and the fierce women who bring them to their knees. When not writing, she can be found daydreaming about owning a beach house, reading, or drinking too much coffee.
You can find her at:
https://www.islavaughnauthor.com

Subscribe to Isla's newsletter for cover reveals, book announcements, and giveaways:
https://bit.ly/IslaVaughnNewsletter

goodreads.com/islavaughn_author
instagram.com/islavaughnauthor
tiktok.com/@islavaughnauthor
bookbub.com/profile/isla-vaughn
facebook.com/author.IslaVaughn
twitter.com/IVaughn_Author